THE FAMILIAR TOUCH

Lynn Lawrence

Rodeo rider Jesse Franklin was once the center of Marlene Whitney's existence, but the passionate affair burned out. Now a sophisticated magazine reporter, Marlene goes back to where it all started and immediately meets Jesse. The old longing comes back strongly and Marlene is tempted to yield to it. But Marlene has changed in the years that have gone by – and Jesse has not. They are worlds apart, and Marlene has made a new life for herself. Can she give it all up for a second chance at love?

SECOND CHANCE AT LOVE
novels in Large Print

Second Chance at Love

LYNN LAWRENCE

The Familiar Touch

John Curley & Associates, Inc.
South Yarmouth, Ma.

Library of Congress Cataloging in Publication Data

Lawrence, Lynn.
  The familiar touch.

  "Published in large print" – Verso t.p.
  "Second chance at love."
  1. Large type books. I. Title.
[PS3562.A913F3   1983]   813'.54   83–7329
ISBN 0–89340–613–9

The Familiar Touch
Lynn Lawrence
SECOND CHANCE AT LOVE Books, published by
Berkely/Jove Publishing Group
Copyright © 1983 by Lynn Lawrence

Published in Large Print by arrangement with Berkely/Jove
Publishing Group.

Distributed in the U.K. and Commonwealth by Magna Print
Books.

Printed in Great Britain

THE FAMILIAR TOUCH

Chapter One

Marlene Whitney's long silky hair tumbled around her face as the silver sports coupe slid to a halt in front of the uniformed man's upheld hand. She saw the policeman shove a black and white striped barricade in front of her car and watched his lips move as he pointed to an overhead banner that rocked softly in the summer breeze. WELCOME TO FRONTIER DAYS RODEO – JULY 19 THRU 26 it read in bold black letters.

"What did you say?" she shouted, rolling down the car window and feeling a gust of hot dry air ruffle her golden brown hair.

"Rodeo parade's fixing to start, ma'am," the officer yelled back with a friendly smile and gestured with his thumb down the main street. Squinting, Marlene could just make out the shifting crowd of horses, cowboys, cowgirls, and a marching band in the bright Texas sun.

"Oh no." She sighed as she plopped

back against the car seat, then glanced at the three-story Texas Star Motel across the main street. Another minute and she would have made it to her destination. Now she was stuck in the car until the parade passed.

How could I have forgotten it was rodeo time, she thought, as she turned off the car motor in frustration. After all, it was the biggest event of the year for her little hometown of Waterford. And being away for six years shouldn't have changed that.

Her intense green eyes scanned the roped-of streets lined with people casually dressed in jeans and Western shirts. A few older women wore simple cotton prints and fanned themselves with cardboard church fans. In the center of town where the large white stone courthouse straddled a green square, children raced around the flagpole just as she had done at their age. It all seemed like a lifetime ago now. Could it really only have been six years since she left?

Funny how time seemed to have slowed to an agonizing crawl after Jesse. Marlene swallowed hard, fighting the surge of memories that rushed into her mind. She shifted her gaze to the milling crowd, but every tall dark-haired man in a cowboy hat sent her heart jumping in anticipation, and her mind hoping he would turn to reveal devastating dark eyes and a flashing grin. But that was impossible. She was certain that Jesse didn't live in Waterford anymore. He'd left a week after she had, to ride the rodeo circuit. A young headstrong ranch hand who saw the rodeo as his only way out of poverty. Breaking ribs, legs, fingers – determined to make it to the top. And he had, from what she read in the articles that were always creeping across her desk at the editorial office in Dallas where she worked.

"No, no, no." she hit her fist against the steering wheel in rhythm to her words as she squeezed her eyes closed and gritted her teeth. "I will *not* think of Jesse. I will *not* think of Jesse." But even as she forced herself to turn away from the crowd, she caught sight of a bright red Texaco sign to her right.

"Everett's Texaco," she sighed with resignation. "I should have known." Six years ago Saturday night meant stopping at Everett's Texaco with Jesse in his gas-guzzling rattletrap pickup with one red and one blue fender. She remembered how

3

Jesse would unwrap his lean sinewy arm from around her shoulder, then swing himself onto the ground, his long legs crammed into indecently tight, faded jeans split at the bottoms to allow his bots to go off and on faster.

A shiver ran through Marlene as she turned away from the gas station. A suffocating panic seized her, so that she instinctively reached for her shoulder bag and a briefcase and opened the car door. Her eyes zoomed in on the only refuge from the past – the new motel across the street that had not even existed six years ago. It would not hold any memories of Jesse. She would go inside and register while her car was stranded behind the barricade.

After sliding gracefully out of the car seat, she closed the door with a soft thud. She heard the noisy commotion of a black and red replica Model T making circles in the street. Raggedy clowns with orange hair and bulbous noses waved and honked as the vehicles popped and sputtered and Marlene waved back with a smile.

Tossing her hair from her creamy smooth face, Marlene slung her purse over one shoulder and clung to the briefcase with her right hand. She walked fast, aware of the curious eyes staring at her slinky green jersey dress and delicate spaghetti-strap high heels.

She had almost reached the other side of the street, hardly noticing the line of horses that she walked behind, when the Model T backfired loudly. A stallion near Marlene neighed in fright and skittered. Marlene gasped, but before she could move, the horse hooves shot out savagely, slamming into her and tumbling her face down to the pavement.

For a brief moment she lay stunned, trying to catch her breath, wondering why she felt no pain other than stinging kneecaps. As she groaned and struggled to her knees, she heard hoofbeats thundering down from an unknown direction. Instinctively she threw her hands over her head and cringed as the hooves cracked louder and closer. Then, from out of nowhere, a strong arm seized her waist from behind and scooped her up to the saddle of the charging horse.

"What are you doing? Put me down!" She tried to pry the lean tanned fingers from her stomach, but failed.

"Didn't I teach you never to walk behind a horse?" a masculine voice asked, followed by a peal of familiar laughter.

Marlene's words of protest froze in her throat and she twisted to face her abductor.

"Jesse!" The word was hardly more than a dry whisper.

"You never were much of a cowgirl,' he said teasingly, his hand possessively increasing the pressure on her stomach.

"That's because the big dumb cowboy that was supposed to be showing me how to ride horses was too busy teaching me other things," she retorted, as she peered into the face above her, devouring the dancing brown eyes and the dark masculine shadow on his firm jaw.

"Ha!" Jesse threw his head back and roared and his arms pulled her closer to his hard, warm body. She responded instinctively by sliding her hands around his back, feeling the dampness of his shirt in the sweltering heat of the day. When he looked at her, his eyes twinkled mischievously. "Same old saucy Marlene."

"I wouldn't bet on that," she whispered. But Jesse apparently didn't notice what she had said, for he continued to flash his white grin, accentuated by a dimple in one cheek, and his hands refused to loosen their grip, even though the large bay stallion

6

underneath his legs shifted and impatiently tried to sidestep in annoyance.

"Speaking of big and dumb," Jesse said, "I used to always make fun of those purses you carried, but looks like that one just saved your life. Or at least it saved you from having some mighty sore ribs."

"Purse?" Her eyes widened until Jesse nodded at the briefcase lying on the street. Its caved-in side clearly showed the imprint of a horseshoe in the leather, and the latch had snapped so that a few papers peeped out. A chill ran over Marlene at the thought of how close she had come to being seriously hurt. She shifted her weight off the saddle horn, which pressed painfully into her thigh. Jesse sensed her discomfort and quickly leaned over, hoisting her to the ground. Then he swung down, his lean muscular thigh rippling as he rested his full weight on the left leg.

Marlene stared at his tight faded jeans and the familiar checked shirt with a bright red bandanna at the neck.

The top two shirt snaps were unfastened to reveal the edge of dark chest hairs, and her fingers began to hunger for the touch of the trim body that stood so close she could feel the heat radiating between them. Jesse removed his hat to wipe his brow, then rolled up each shirt shirt sleeve to the elbow, exposing sinewy tanned forearms. His tall frame cast a shadow over Marlene's slender form, making her even more acutely aware of his masculine presence.

She hesitated, searching for the words to express the emotions swelling inside her. As the silence lengthened, his dark eyes locked with hers and something passed between them – something like a warm summer breeze stirring a bed of burned-out coals to reveal glowing embers underneath. As Marlene stared into the bottomless depths of his eyes, she saw a battle raging fiercely. In her heart she knew that he was reliving their old love and arguments and last day together. Her heart began to pound within her chest and her fingers trembled in anticipation. Then, suddenly, a fire snapped in his eyes and he turned to the horse and began adjusting the saddle gear.

Marlene stifled a cry and stepped closer to him, placing her hand absentmindedly on the beautiful quarter horse, stroking the sleek neck with her fingers, but hardly aware of the warm, silky hide.

"Jesse? Are you in Waterford for the rodeo?" she asked in her friendliest voice.

"Nope," he replied curtly as he loosened the saddle girth. "Not necessarily."

"I heard you almost won the world championship two years ago. Nobody deserved it more than you."

Jesse shrugged and skillfully tightened the girth, looping the band through the metal hoops with firm, powerful jerks. Marlene saw a slight smile touch his lips.

"Sounds like you've been following my career real close. I didn't think you wanted to have anything to do with me or rodeos."

The words struck Marlene like a blast of frigid air, and she felt the blood drain from her cheeks, then return in a surge of fiery heat.

"Six years is a long time to harbor a grudge, Jesse," she replied softly, moving her arm and placing a hand caressingly on his sleeve. She watched his face cloud, then saw the clenched teeth and taut jawline relax as he turned to face her. The dark eyes bored into her for a moment, then he smiled slightly and thumped his hat brim up with his forefinger.

"Yep, guess you're right. And, besides, parts of me never held a grudge in the first place." He pulled her closer and his arms encircled her waist. For a brief instant his eyes searched hers, saw the welcoming glow, then his lips took hers, pressing with a savage tenderness that sent a wave of ecstasy through her body and her heart racing out of control. She felt the pressure of his desire against her body as the kiss lingered, lifting her to another plane of hunger, making her arms respond by circling his broad back. When they separated, her breath came in short ragged bursts.

"Does that mean you forgive me?"

Jesse shrugged. "Why not? I'd almost come to the natural conclusion that you'd never come back – that you got married or something and didn't care about any of this small-town living anymore." He waved a tanned well-shaped hand over the parade line of horses and the old courthouse and milling crowd. "But I guess if you came all the way back here just to this little hometown rodeo, well, how could I *not* forgive you." He pulled her close again and buried his face against her neck. Marlene felt her face going pale and she swallowed hard as her eyes took in the smashed briefcase full of work papers. A wave of guilt washed over her at the thought that she had come to Waterford solely on business – that she had completely forgotten about the rodeo. But far worse than that, Jesse acted as if he had no knowledge of her previous marriage. She had written him a long letter, begging his forgiveness, pleading for another try. But getting no response left her with no other alternative than to marry the young man she thought she could learn to love.

I had been a mistake, she knew now. And surely Jesse would understand. Marlene's logic coaxed her lips to speak and take the consequences, but her thundering heart and trembling fingers told her that now was not the time or place. She knew Jesse's hotheadedness too well to risk this precious moment of reunion by explaining the errors of her past. Maybe later when the moon was glowing in his dark eyes and soft music lulled his senses.

As Jesse released her, Marlene quickly dropped to her knees and began shoving the protruding sheets back inside the briefcase.

"Here, let me help you," Jesse offered and he knelt beside her.

"No, no, that's all right. It's nothing," she stammered, while her fingers shook violently as she tried to fasten the latches.

11

Jesse examined her with a perplexed expression, then pried the case from her hands.

"This latch is busted. Looks like the hoof clipped it. Let me try something." He stood up, reached into his jeans pocket to retrieve a pocketknife, then knelt again.

"Jesse, really, you don't have to bother. I-I don't need this fixed right now."

"Hush up." He began bending the metal latch with his knife blade. As he turned the briefcase on its end, the papers started coming out again of the partial opening. Jesse looked at the white sheets, then glanced at her and gently tugged the papers free.

"I thought this was a funny-looking purse," he mumbled as he began reading the top page.

"Jesse, please, let me explain." Marlene tried to take the paper from his hand, but he moved it out of her reach and read on.

"No need to, Marlene," His voice had turned to ice and he shoved the sheets back into the briefcase. "So, you're in town on business, huh?" He slammed the case shut, pushed it into her hands, and stood up. "I should have known it. I should have known it." He jerked his hat down low on his brow

12

and grabbed the saddle horn.

"Jesse, please, don't be mad. I didn't know the rodeo was going on or that you were here in town. But if I had, I swear I would have found you." She took his arm gently.

"Ha!" Suddenly he swirled around and dug his hands into her shoulders. "Why didn't you tell me you were here on some reporter's assignment in the first place? Why'd you let me make a genuine fool outa myself – talking about taking you back and forgiveness." Sparks flew from his dark eyes.

"Well, I see six years hasn't simmered down that temper of yours any," Marlene said, yanking her arms free and rubbing the spots that ached from his rough touch.

"And you're just as sneaky as ever."

"Sneaky!" she protested.

"Conniving. Always using your beauty and your body to get what you want from me."

"What are you talking about? When did – "

"Just then. Got me so hot I almost dragged you into the back alley over there."

"You're the one who kissed me first, you fool."

"Yep, I'm a fool all right. Thinking you cared enough to ever come back to a one-horse town like Waterford after tasting the good life of the big city."

As he lifted his weight into the stirrup, then gracefully swung his right leg over the saddle and slid into it with a slap, Marlene shouted up, "You're not just a stubborn mule, Jesse Franklin, you're a stubborn mule with blinders on your eyes." Her voice trembled with emotion and the tall figure towering above her began to blur through her watery vision. She saw the dark horse dance in place a few seconds, then suddenly pivot on his hind legs as Jesse swung him back around.

"Ah, hell, don't start that crying stuff."

"I'm not crying," she denied, her chin fighting not to quiver and her nose trying not to sniff. She leaned down and scooped up a tube of lipstick that had rolled out of her handbag, turning her back on Jesse. She sniffed and pawed at her wet eyes angrily, determined not to give him the satisfaction of knowing she was hurt and bent on going directly to the motel before another thing interrupted. But when she rose and turned, Jesse's solid form blocked her path.

"Come here. Don't cry. I can't stand to see you cry, you know that." His arms reached out to comfort her, but she pushed them away.

"I don't need your sympathy," she replied indignantly.

"Well, you're losing it mighty fast," he said, grabbing her arm and leading her to the curb, then yanking a clean white handkerchief from his back pocket. "Here.' He pushed it under her nose, but she shoved it back at him.

"I don't want it,' she hissed, then as she felt her nose start to run, she quickly seized it from his fingers. "I changed my mind."

"That figures,' he mumbled. After dabbing at her eyes, she handed the soiled cloth back. In a softer tone of voice, he asked, "Say, where're you staying anyhow?"

"None of your business."

"Ah, sh... Come on, Marlene." He knocked his hat back on his forehead and gave her a pleading look.

"The Texas Star Motel.' She nodded at the squatty glass and brick building. "I'll be there two days at least." She looked into his face with hope in her eyes. "Are you staying there, too?"

"Nope." Jesse squared his shoulders and gave the milling crowd a quick scan, as if looking for something. After a few seconds, he quickly dropped his gaze and smiled lightly. "But maybe we'll run into each other again before you leave."

Before Marlene's heart had time to sink, the sound of a man's gravelly voice cut through the air.

"C'mon, Jess, boy, the parade's a-fixing to start. We're waiting on you. Can't start without the Texas flag."

Marlene swirled to face an older man of indeterminable age, a small and skinny man, with a large silver and turquoise belt buckle hanging obtrusively on his tiny waist. From his left jaw there protruded a wad of chewing tobacco, and his leathery face cracked into a million wrinkles as he squinted his deep gray eyes.

"Freddy!" she exclaimed with a broad smile.

The man stopped in his tracks, glared a moment, then shoved a livers-spotted hand covered with wiry gray hairs toward her.

16

"Well, I'll be doggoned! If it ain't Jesse's girl. What in tarnation are you doing here, sugar lamb?' He shook her hand firmly, then pulled her near enough to place a tobacco-flavored kiss on her smooth cheek. Then he held her at arm's length and winked as his merry old eyes danced up and down her shapely figure. "Um, um. Now didn't you turn out to be a looker. What're you doing here, anyhow? In town for the rodeo? And to pay old Jesse a visit?" He winked again, this time at Jesse, and gave the tall cowboy an elbow jab to the stomach.

"Guess again, Freddy," Jesse corrected, his dark eyes never leaving Marlene's face. She quickly looked back at the short man to avoid the penetrating glare.

"Uh, actually, Freddy, I work for *Texas People Magazine* now and I'm writing a story on quarter-horse ranches. I'll be starting my research with the Yancy Ranch." Marlene formed a quick mental image of Freddy's bosses. Sam and Jewel Yancy, always laughing, joking, and treating her like their own daughter. The Yancys had been the closest thing to parents that Jesse ever knew, and he had been like a son to them, though he slept in the bunkhouse with the rest of the ranch hands.

"*Texas People Magazine,*" Freddy said, scratching his prickly chin. "As I recollect the boss-lady takes that one, don't she, Jesse?"

Jesse didn't reply. He seemed absorbed in deep thought, his eyes never wavering from Marlene. Freddy shrugged off Jesse's silence.

"Well, anyhow, Jewel's gonna bust a garter when she finds out you're back in town. She was plumb wild about you, angel."

"I really liked her to, Freddy. And I'd like to interview you when you have time – about the horses and how you run the ranch hands. And take a few pictures of the boys at work."

"Ah, shoot!" Freddy chuckled as he removed his buff-colored straw hat and ran his fingers through his thinning sandy hair. He shifted the wad of tobacco to the other side of his jaw, then cleared his throat. "Say, you're going to the rodeo this evening, I reckon?"

"You ought to know by now that Marlene hates rodeos." Jesse's icy words pierced the conversation, taking Marlene by surprise. She glanced up to see his taut lips and searing eyes. her heart throbbed in her temples so fiercely that she could not think clearly, though she longed to tell him, to explain very logically and coolly, that she had nothing against rodeos. She only hated them because she was forced to watch him, she was petrified that he might be maimed, broken, or killed. Even now after six years, the very thought of seeing him on a bucking horse again put a tight hard knot in her stomach. Freddy's worn voice was a welcome relief.

"Ah, I don't believe that, Jess. Why, this little gal traveled all over the state with you when you was a young, ornery colt. She musta seen every rodeo in the state." He put a calloused hand on her silky sleeve. "It'll break my old heart in two if you don't come."

With a deepening dread, Marlene forced her eyes to meet the dark ones above her. At the expression she saw, her heart lurched. Whether it was hatred or pain, she couldn't be positive. But one thing was sure: Jesse's tone and his tight jawline told her that she was unwelcome in his life. The brief moment of joy at the first encounter had apparently drowned beneath a torrent

19

of old, painful memories. Obviously he still harbored resentment because of their breakup, and any thought of a possible rekindling of their relationship, even just as mere friends, seemed all too remote right now in the glaring summer sun. Marlene tore her eyes away from Jesse's face and tried to force a smile for the short foreman.

"No, Freddy, I'm sorry, but I can't go. I'm too tired."

The little cowboy glared up at her in disbelief, then turned to Jesse.

"Well, boy, ain't you gonna say something?" he asked blatantly.

"Yes, I'll say something," Jesse replied curtly, then pivoted and swung up on his horse. "Good-bye." With one last dart at Marlene, he shoved the hat brim low on his brow, then jerked his knees against the horse's ribs and charged off.

Chapter Two

Marlene watched Jesse riding away at a gallop, feeling a lump rise to her throat as if she'd swallowed a large sharp rock. When she turned to Freddy, the old man was shaking his head.

"Fool boy's acting like he's addled. Don't let him upset you, dumpling. He's just got a sore head from knocking noggins with a yearling bull yesterday."

"I understand," she replied softly, her eyes still attached to the dark stallion and tall rider that by now had pulled to a stop beside another dark horse ridden by a redheaded girl. The girl, who carried the American flag, handed Jesse the Texas flag, mounted on a long pole. She must have questioned Jesse on his whereabouts for suddenly she swirled around in the saddle and stared intently at Marlene. Even from that distance Marlene caught the shimmer and sparkle of the silver sequins on the beautiful blue and white cowgirl outfit.

"Well, sugar lamb, I for one am pure

21

delighted to see you back in town, and just in the knick of time, if you ask me," Freddy said, stepping out of the way of a horse hurrying to join the line.

"What do you mean?" Marlene asked, tearing her gaze from Jesse to look down into the gray eyes.

"That there little sassy redhead's been doing some mighty strong figuring lately, and it all adds up to her being Mrs. Jesse Franklin. And Jesse's just stubborn enough and bamboozled enough that he might do it. But now that he's got a real woman to compare that little spitfire to, there shouldn't be no contest."

"But I'm not here to – " Marlene's words were interrupted by a sharp whistle blast.

"Gotta vamos, dumpling. Catch you at the ranch later on." Without waiting for her reply, Freddy put his hand to his hat and scooted across the street in time to mount a large gray mare. Horses shifted their legs, and as the Texas and American flags moved, the parade line reeled forward. Like an undulating ocean wave, every cowboy hat in the crowd swept off and every hand tenderly covered its master's heart as the flags passed by.

The first line of horses clomped by,

permeating the air with the odor of hoof polish, leather, and sweat. The riders all wore matching brownchaps with bright red shirts and black string ties, and the words "Sheriff's Posse" on their backs. The heavy clunk of horseshoes on the pavement intermingled with the creaking saddles and stirrups and the soft jingle of bits and bridles decorated with shiny silver conchas. Some animals grew restless, tossing their heads as they sidestepped, chomping the bits, and shifting impatiently at the slow-moving pace.

Soon Marlene heard the boom of a brass drum followed by the familiar brassy sound of a marching high school band. In a few minutes the methodic snap of boots cracked the asphalt, and a line of majorettes pranced into view, twirling shiny silver batons. Their bright blue satin blouses contrasted sharply with the white thigh-high skirts, and the silky tassles on the white boots swung in rhythm to the bouncing young hips.

Was I ever that young and prissy, Marlene asked herself, as the girls passed by, each one forcing herself to smile even as the sweat dripped down her face. The leader turned and maneuvered in the middle of the street with confident agility, the silver stick spinning around her body with lightning-fast accuracy and flying high into the air from time to time, but landing securely back in her nimble fingers.

Marlene often thought about the fateful day seven years ago when she had led the row of majorettes in this same rodeo parade. If she'd caught her baton that day, she never would have met Jesse, never would have known the thrill of his arms, or the heartache of the separation that still haunted her dreams.

But when Marlene's baton had flown high into that July sky, the sun had temporarily blinded her and she had lost track of its path. In cruel mockery the silver rod with its white rubber ends bounded down the street behind her and smacked into the legs of the first horse it came to in the parade. The animal skittered and reared, its hooves smashing down on the wand. In embarrassment and humiliation, Marlene dashed from the parade, running as fast as her booted feet would allow down steep, hilly Brazos Street until she came to the winding creek that snuggled at its base.

She would have leaped in, except that the

waters were a mere algae-infested slimy trickle. Sitting on the concrete embankment, sobbing, she hardly heard the long-legged black horse stop in front of her. She looked up at the young man in the saddle and saw a pair of immensely dark brown eyes, glimmering velvet soft with compassion. The lips of the tanned face remained silent as he handed down the ruined baton, his long, strong fingers wrapped around the delicate feminine plaything as if it were a knight's lance.

He tried to console her and at first she would not let him, but his vote of confidence in her talent and his warm heart finally won her over. When her tears were dried and a smile touched her lips, he extended his hand.

"Come on," he said with a warm smile, "I'll take you back." She shook her head no, but he leaned down and scooped her up in his strong arms, placing her in front of him on the saddle. With his arms wrapped around her waist, she could feel the warmth of his faded jeans pressing against her bare thighs and the firmness of his chest against her back. She thought she could hear the thumping of his heart through the checked shirt, but decided it was definitely her own heartbeat.

That was how it had all started, and by the end of the night they danced on the rope-off street around the old courthouse square in each other's arms, watching the stars twinkle above. When they parted, he said, "You want to be my girl?" and Marlene's heart was never the same.

Marlene blinked rapidly to bring the present parade back into focus, only to find that it was almost over. The Model T made circles in the street, while the clowns honked and tossed out candy behind the last string of horses – beautifully matched palominos with long platinum-blond tails that almost dragged the ground like combed silk.

With a sniff and toss of her head, Marlene slung her purse over her shoulder and, clutching the ruined briefcase, she returned to her car, then drove to the motel parking lot.

The motel lobby sparkled with the look and smell of newness. Fresh potted palms graced the entrance and perfectly matched sofas and chairs of conservative blue and gold patterns sat austerely in the corner of the room.

Marlene tugged at her dress, hoping it

decently covered her scraped knee and ruined stockings, but as the receptionist glanced down at her she knew it was hopeless.

"I'd like a single room, please," Marlene told the young clerk at the desk.

"Certainly." He quickly and efficiently passed the registration form to Marlene and watched as she signed her name. He flipped the paper around, then cocked one eyebrow as he read the signature.

"You're Marlene Whitney?" he asked, a little cautiously.

"Yes. Is something wrong?"

"Why, no, ma'am. It's just that a reservation's already been made for you. It's not necessary for you to fill out all these papers." He tore them up with a smile.

"But ... how? I mean, I didn't even know I was going to stay here until a few minutes ago. I didn't even know this motel was here. This lot was nothing but an abandoned warehouse the last time I lived in Waterford."

The clerk chuckled dryly. "Well, there's a registration in your name. Room 301, our very best. The gentleman who called seemed very sure of himself and – "

"Gentleman?" Marlene's eyebrows flew up.

"Why yes. His name was . . . uh, let me see." The clerk thumbed through the file until he found Marlene's reservation, and he quickly scanned it. "Yes. His name was Vaughn Casstevens. If there's a problem, Miss Whitney . . ."

Marlene expelled a long sigh of relief, then smiled.

"Of course. I should have known. Mr. Casstevens is my boss. I'm in town for business, and I guess he assumed that I would be staying at the best motel in town." She laughed lightly before adding, "Since it's *his* expense account."

The clerk nodded in understanding, then, as Marlene turned to go, he called out, "Miss Whitney, I almost forgot to tell you. Mr. Casstevens also left you a telephone message." He reached under the counter and withdrew a sealed envelope, handed it to Marlene, then banged on the desk bell. A Mexican boy in a bright red uniform stepped up seemingly from out of nowhere and quickly and skillfully carried her sparse luggage to the elevator.

As he unlocked Room 301 the luscious smell of roses and honeysuckle rushed through the door. Stepping inside, Marlene

28

caught sight of the large vase of flowers that literally smothered the top of the small occasional table in the center of the sitting area.

"How beautiful!" she exclaimed, walking quickly over to bury her nose in the fragrant bouquet. "What service!"

"They're not from the motel, ma'am. These are a gift, ordered by someone. Here's the card." He found the small card hidden in the honeysuckle and handed it to Marlene. She moved her lips slightly as she read the words.

"Beautiful women should have beautiful flowers. Love, Vaughn."

Marlene smiled softly, then dug into her purse for a tip. After removing her shoes and replacing the ruined hose, she settled down in the plush overstuffed tweed chair near a tiny balcony that overlooked the motel's swimming pool. Though it was 95 degrees outside, the room was chilly because of an overactive air conditioner, so she opened the French doors and drew back the curtains to let in some warmth and sunlight. Slowly she leaned back and closed her eyes. Her dark lids became the canvas on which she painted the picture of Vaugh Casstevens, her editor. She saw him clearly: average height, blond hair, sharp blue eyes, and a pallor that came from years of dedicated office work. What an irony, she thought. For, thanks to an inheritance from an oil and real estate family, Vaughn could have easily taken part in the endless stream of parties and wild escapades of his wealthy Dallas peers. But instead he led the sedate hard-driving life of an up-and-coming businessman whose subdued gray suits and impeccable gentleman's manners often left a more lasting impression on women than any outlandish cowboy suit or python-skin boots.

Few reporters, secretaries, photographers – or any other employee – could endure the hard-nosed precision demanded by Vaughn, who himself was an expert at every phase of the magazine business. Marlene, however, seemed to thrive on the challenge of his demands, and they worked together very well. But she had never thought of Vaughn as anything but a boss and friend. His romantic overtures, like his quiet unimposing clothes, were refined and so subtle that Marlene went into shock when he proposed one night while they worked late to meet a deadline.

At first she was pleased, but as the

prospects of another marriage stared her in the face, she panicked and became nervous to the point of neglecting her work. Vaughn knew about her first marriage and he even knew about Jesse, but nothing dissuaded his persistent nature. Vaughn wasn't stubborn in the sense that Jesse was, but simply used to getting what he wanted.

Marlene rose and walked to the balcony. A tall young oak tree cast its welcome shadow over her face, sending dappled streaks over the smooth lightly tanned features and serious green eyes. She stared at the shimmering blue pool waters, not seeing the squealing children or sleek women soaking up the late-afternoon sun. The waters only reminded her of the cool blue eyes of Vaughn Casstevens.

The whole idea of the quarter-horse article was his, and, she knew in her heart, just a test of her loyalty to him.

"You're getting all spooky-eyed," he'd said as he plopped the assignment sheet on her desk. "Take a couple of days to go to the country to do this one." And the next day he came to her apartment to say good-bye, carried her luggage to her car, and when she found that the battery was dead, quickly tossed her the keys to his sleek silver sports car without another thought.

"Think things over while you're out there in the cow pastures picking your way around the buffalo chips," he'd said with a laugh. "Go ahead and visit that cowboy you were stuck on years ago and get him out of your system. I know that's what's putting your decision off. There's nothing on earth like teenage love, but you're no high school majorette anymore. You're a woman and not getting any younger. You go back to him and you'll find that living on red beans and corn bread has a way of putting the fire out of your britches."

Marlene felt a little twinge of irritation creeping over her at the thought of Vaughn's confidence, but in her heart she knew he was right. She could never be happily married to any man until she was sure that Jesse was out of her life forever. She had already made that mistake once and was determined never to repeat it.

Her fingers trembled and she suddenly realized that her heart was pounding at the mere thought of Jesse. With a little moan she pushed away from the balcony and returned to the room. After a moment's hesitation, she picked up the envelope on the lamp stand, turned it over several times, then ripped it open.

"Marlene:" it read. "By the time you read this message you'll probably have walked around the old hometown, weepy-eyed because nothing's the same, and brokenhearted because no one recognized you. And I hope you've run into the old cowboy lover, saw his potbelly, sickly wife, and six kids and now you're ready to come home to Dallas where you belong. Something's come up here more important than the ranch story. I need you back in the office by Monday morning. Call me as soon as you arrive at the motel. Love, Vaughn."

A deep sigh of frustration and dis-appointment rose from Marlene's lungs as her fingers slowly crumpled the note into a tight ball. She stood in the middle of the room, red-faced, annoyance prickling the back of her neck at the thought of the wasted trip to Waterford. It wasn't like Vaughn to pull a trick of any kind, but this was certainly what it looked like.

With all the composure she possessed, Marlene placed a long distance call to the Dallas office. Vaughn's voice was warm and full of self-satisfaction.

"Marlene! Your call is right on time."

"Vaughn, what are you trying to do, give

me jet lag? I just got here and now you say I'm supposed to come back."

"Yes, but . . ."

"But you promised me this story and even insinuated it was to be a little vacation."

"Vacation?" He chuckled. "What in tarnation is there to do in Waterford, Texas, beside dip snuff and play forty-two?"

Marlene laughed herself. If Vaughn's highbrow friends and relatives knew he had knowledge of such countrified points, they'd disown him.

"Well, as a matter of fact, the annual Frontier Days Rodeo is starting tonight and – "

"Rodeo?" Vaughn's voice turned to ice. "I see. So you've met the old cowboy lover, haven't you?"

Marlene gripped the receiver and slowly lowered herself to the edge of the bed.

"Y-yes," she replied softly.

"Well?"

"I-I don't understand what you mean. . . ." She stammered to a halt.

"Oh yes you do. Is everything patched up between you two? Is he married now?"

"No to both questions. It was an

accident I even saw him, and I doubt we'll see each other again." She waited for a response, but the seconds ticked away, leaving her uneasy. "Vaughn, are you still there?"

"Yes, of course."

"Well, I'd like to visit the Yancy Ranch. I know there's a good story here. The local color, the traditions. These ranchers are a dying breed in Texas."

"And while you're at the Yancy Ranch, you'll just happen to visit with the cowboy too, I guess."

"No, you don't have to be concerned about that. Our encounter wasn't exactly friendly."

"Really?" she detected a tone of pleasure in his voice and crossed her fingers. "Okay, Marlene. Do what you can with the story in two days. Just be back by eight A.M. Monday. But, it's not an authorized assignment, so you'll have to pay for the expenses out of your own pocket. If I decide to use it, then I'll reimburse you. Good-bye."

The receiver clicked in her ear before Marlene could reply, and as she clunked it back into the cradle, a surge of anger swept over her. With a scream, she tossed the

35

crumpled message across the room with all her strength, disappointed at the weak scrape it made on the front wall. Suddenly she grabbed the two unpacked suitcases and went out of the room, slamming the door behind her.

"Miss Whitney!" The desk clerk's eyes widened and his mouth dropped open as he saw a flash of green dress coming from the elevator. "Is something wrong?"

"No," she explained. "I need to pay for a long-distance phone call. Nothing was wrong with the room, but I'm checking out. A personal matter." She didn't dare tell him that her own bank account wouldn't allow this nice motel. She would have to search the edges of the town for something within her meager budget. As she waited for the clerk to figure out the charge for her phone call, she looked at the swimming pool wistfully and smelled the aroma of food drifting from the kitchen.

When she was in the silver sports coupe, her eyes rested on the inert steering wheel covered in expensive leather. The simplest thing to do would be return to Dallas and forget the ranch story, Freddy, the Yancys, and Jesse.

"If I only could forget you, Jesse," she softly muttered, jamming the keys into the ignition and whipping the wheel around.

Within minutes she was on the main highway again, driving in the direction away from Dallas. As she whizzed past the town limits down the old, worn Highway 80, a green and red neon sign caught her attention. A smile crept over her lips, and she slowed the car and turned into the gravelled drive of the white stucco motel. It was surrounded by huge prickly pear cacti and hunks of petrified wood arranged in haphazard fashion near a stagnant swimming pool. Out front, near the highway, stood a giant metal bow-legged cowboy whose red shirt and blue pants and ten gallon hat were outlined in neon lights. His right arm, with the thumb sticking out like that of a hitchhiker, had once moved in slow mechanical ease, beckoning passing travelers. Now his arm lay silent, and sparrows' nests cascaded from his shoulders in dirty brown heaps – ever since the new Interstate had replaced old Highway 80 as the main route eastward. An eerie feeling crept over Marlene as she stopped the car and climbed out onto the gravel and dirt strip in front of the shabby office. A light was on inside, but a handwritten note announced that the attendant was out to supper. Through the broken venetian blind slats she could see a pile of *Playboy* magazines and dirty coffee cups.

With a sigh Marlene turned around. Down the highway she could make out a familiar pair of headlights in the evening dusk. They had been following her since she had left the motel. Probably just someone going to see the rodeo, she told herself, as she strolled around the white stucco complex, pausing to smell some red roses that rambled carelesly up the side of one unit. She glanced at her watch. The note had not said what time the attendant would return, but from the looks of business she doubted that he would be in any hurry.

Reluctantly she walked back to the silver car. She was just reaching for the door handle when the headlights swung into the parking lot only a few feet from her. It was a blue truck that ground to a halt in the driveway and blocked her exit. Panic quickly filled Marlene when she saw a man's silhouette in the cab and her heart thumped louder as the truck door crashed open and she heard a man's voice declare: "I've got you now!"

Chapter Three

But once the light from the pick up cab flooded over the man, a deep sigh of relief tumbled through Marlene's body. She glanced at the side of the blue truck and saw the words "Yancy Ranch" and the ranch's horse head emblem circled by a horseshoe. Behind the pickup was a four-stall horse trailer of the same shade of blue. She quickly returned her gaze to the friendly face of Freddy, who was grinning broadly at her.

"You doggoned little spitfire. I never seen anybody skeedaddle down the road so fast. Made my old Chevy feel like it was standing still." He chuckled as he climbed down from the cab and spat a brown stream toward the nearest clump of cactus.

"Freddy, I didn't know that was you following me. What's wrong?"

"Well, I've been thinking 'bout you and the rodeo. Now, I know it ain't none of my cotton-picking business, but I just can't stand to see you not going to the rodeo just because you figure Jesse don't want you there. Just think of all the colorful folks you could take pictures of, and the yarns from the old codgers. It'd sure make a good story for that magazine. Might even win you a blue ribbon." He winked.

"I'm not here to do a story on the rodeo," Marlene replied coolly.

Freddy shifted the tobacco wad to the other side of his jaw, then squinted into her face. After a long pause, he lifted a finger and pointed it at her nose.

"I've made up my mind that you're going to the rodeo or else."

Marlene felt the blood drain from her face. "Or else what, Freddy?" she asked, crossing her arms and peering down at the short man.

"Or else I ain't gonna tell you one galderned fact nor tall tale 'bout the quarter-horse ranching business. You'll just have to find somebody else." His face remained taut and firm, the jaw set at a stubborn angle. Their eyes locked for a moment, then with a shake of her head, Marlene let out a long sigh.

"All right, Freddy, you've convinced me with your indisputable Irish charm. I'll go. But don't expect me to go behind the chutes or anything else. I'll just sit quietly in the stand and watch. Then tmorrow I'll get those yarns and the interview."

"Mighty fine, honey pot. Now, we'd best light a shuck outa here. It's almost time for the rodeo to start." He was grinning from ear to ear.

Marlene waved at him, then crawled into the silver car, wondering why she was doing this, but feeling better for the moment. She quickly eased the car back to the highway and plunged into the evening dusk toward the rodeo grounds. Cars were inching by the gates and parking on a gravel lot. She bought a ticket and was thankful that no one recognized her, though every face looked familiar to her. She found a cozy spot in a removed corner where not too many people were sitting.

The smell of earth and manure from the stables mingled with the tang of mustard and popcorn aroma to create a special blend that only a rodeo could possess. The chutes on the far side were no longer bright red. They were now white, though an occasional nick or scratch showed the rust-color of yesterday. The bleachers were old, but sturdy, and below them Marlene could see children dashing about and couples trying to sneak kisses. The whinnying of horses and bellowing of cattle sent a wave of nostalgia through Marlene. The sun was below the horizon now and the first weak stars twinkled in the rapidly cooling sky. Mosquitoes hummed, and people passed a can of insect repellent down the bleacher rows.

The rodeo was a small one, with mostly local townsmen and farmers as the audience. But it was, in a way, far more lively than the larger, more sophisticated commercial rodeos with electronic billboards and piped music that the big cities offered. The announcer's twang and country wit would not have meant much to most city dwellers. The man seemed to know every bull and horse personally, and every contestant, calling them by their first names, making cracks about their personalities and families and love lives. The audience snickered constantly, and Marlene soon relaxed, tucking her stockinged shoeless feet underneath her like a schoolgirl on the gym floor, and thinking how easy it was to fall back into the frame of mind of earlier years, as if nothing had ever happened.

The first event, calf roping, was fast and

furious. How young the boys looked to her now. Could Jesse have ever been that wild and reckless? Had time flown that fast? Rodeos had a timelessness about them that no other sport could claim. The clothes – jeans, hats, boots, checked shirts – stayed eternally the same. The horses still bucked today as they did a hundred years ago, and the bull still pawed the soft earth and snorted with glinty black eyes radiating hatred from a lowered head. And the music of fiddles or sweet guitars that floated over the stands moaned out the ageless tale of cowboy woes. Only the parking lot, filled with late-model cars and oversized pickup cabs with doubled wheels in the back gave away the secret of passing time.

Next came the bull dogging event. Small, wiry, lean men who looked as if they couldn't lift a hammer, much less tackle 1500 pounds of black bull meat to the sandy arena floor, performed. The crowd groaned as each man leaned his weight into the bull, twisting the stubborn head at an agonizing angle until the horn tips touched the ground. The next event was barrel racing, then pole bending. The young cowgirls slapped their speeding mounts fiercely, yelling and screaming like Annie

Oakley. The winner of these events, a pretty girl of about twenty with sleek red hair, waved and smiled to the audience as if she knew each one personally. During intermission the clowns rode about on miniature donkeys and ponies. After intermission, the show resumed with saddle bronc riding, then bull riding. Bull riding was nerve-racking for the bulls were exceptionaly jittery, perhaps because of the hovering thunderclouds that had been gradually building on the horizon, and the cracks of thunder and lightning that were steadily increasing. People began to mill about, casting their eyes upward, mumbling, praying the last event would come before they were forced to run for cover.

Marlene gathered her purse, in case she might need to make a mad dash in the drenching rain. She knew all too well how fast these summer storms brewed, dumped inches of cold, big drops, then vanished, leaving the earth sweet, clean, and just as hot as before within an hour. But as the loudspeaker crackled out the next event, bareback riding, she sat back down. It had been Jesse's strongest event. He'd won prizes for it from small towns all over the state, and had lined his bunk with the ribbons, trophies, and belt buckles.

The first rider rode well and good-humoredly took the jibes from the announcer when he landed in an awkward position before the sound of the buzzer. The next rider was a tall teenager who was tossed off quickly, rolling to a motionless halt after slamming into the earth. As the two assistants rushed to him, he sat up and limped to the gates. The crowd gave him a warm ovation, though the youth couldn't hide his disappointment. The loudspeaker crackled again and the announcer's voice cut into the mosquito-infested night air.

"And now folks, riding Texas Twister, our own home-town boy, Jesse Franklin." The crowd burst into applause and Marlene sat up with a bolt, feeling the color drain from her face. The announcer continued in a warm, proud voice. "Jesse's won so many prizes I'd have to be talking till midnight to name 'em all, folks. But you know that. He's not doing this for money tonight, just for fun. Some fun, huh, getting your head busted open and your bottom bounced like a yo-yo. Old Jesse says if he can stay on that ornery knot-headed cayuse tonight, he'll donate twice the prize money to the rodeo funds." The crowd cheered again. "And ... if he gets thrown, he'll donate four times the money. Well, now, old Texas Twister ain't never been ridden the limit. Not even by Jesse when he was a young whippersnapper. So here goes. Good luck, Jess, you'll need it."

The gate swung open and Marlene caught her breath as the giant gray horse with black mane and tail leaped from the chute, twisting and jerking and writhing his huge body with crushing dexterity. He tucked his head between his front legs in fierce concentration, and his hind legs thrust out wildly, until at one point his entire massive body left the ground, all the while twisting and circling like a gyroscope gone haywire. The crowd stood on its feet screaming and roaring as the tall lean man lay back, his spur-tipped heels jabbing the gray shoulders mercilesely, his left hand gripping the rope and his right hand flaying high above his head. His body leaned with the animal's, and turned as the horse turned, as if in some kind of secret communication with the gray beast. His grace was breathtaking. The seconds were transformed into an eternity, space and time frozen as man and horse became a new creature, neither man nor horse, but a single gyrating, leaping thing beneath the mellow lights of the arena. Marlene rose to her feet, her lips parted and her eyes absorbing the beauty of the scene below. Jesse's hat flew off, freeing a tangle of dark hair that bobbed in rhythm with the rock and roll of the gray body beneath his legs. When Marlene saw Jesse slipping to one side, she glanced at the overhead clock dashing off the seconds, and her hands formed fists and suddenly her own lips were screaming, her throat growing raw from the vibrations ripping through it.

"Hold on, Jesse! Hold on!" Her voice rocked the cool night air, and she was unaware that the first large drops of cold rain had splattered her face. No one cared, no one budged from his standing position, even as the arena below suddenly leaped to life with great silver sheets of rain.

"Ride 'im, Jesse!" the crowd chanted, pounding fists into shoulders. And suddenly, as the wet body of the horse yanked a final wicked and sinuous time, the buzzer sounded and Jesse lost hold of the slippery rope. As his body soared through the air, the gray horse rammed his hooves at the passing form in a final symbol of hatred toward the man who had at last defeated him. The crowd, seeing Jesse slammed to the wet dirt, lying motionless, oohed and groaned in sympathy. A bevy of cowhands swarmed over to the silent form and rolled it over.

As the crowd ran for cover and men lifted Jesse up, the announcer remained deadly quiet. When he finally spoke, his voice was subdued and his words no longer witty.

"Rodeo's over for tonight, folks." A loud crackle, then eerie silence followed.

Marlene remained standing, unaware of the people pushing by her, stumbling over her legs. She only saw the men carrying the limp body away and felt a mixture of hot tears and cold rain dripping down her cheeks. She blinked rapidly, then pushed the drenched bangs away from her forehead. Watching Jesse being lifted into the ambulance, a pale purple station wagon that also served as a hearse for the local funeral home, she felt a shiver running wildly down her spine.

This can't be happening, she thought. Not again. Standing there in the bleachers, her brain numb, the pit of her stomach felt heavy and rolling as Jesse's limp form was carried off. It was the nightmare she'd lived over and over for six years, the memory of that last night, that last rodeo she attended. That was the night something finally snapped inside her, releasing a beast that roared and screamed, pleaded and begged the pale and weak Jesse in the hospital waiting room to give it up. But all in vain. Their passion, their love, their engagement – all got lost in the fiery words that flew between them. And he had said softly, "Don't let it end this way," but it did. And when his warm fingers slipped from hers as they wheeled him down the icy sterile hall, a piece of Marlene Whitney's heart defiantly broke away with him.

Marlene felt a sharp pain in her throat as she swallowed. Suddenly, without command, her legs began climbing frantically down the stands. Gripping her high heels in one hand, she felt runners popping up the backs of her legs when her feet caught on the rough wood of the old bleachers. On solid ground again, she broke into a desperate run for the back of the arena where the stock was kept.

Her green eyes darted over the ocean of white, black, and tan cowboy hats and endless stream of leather belts with great silver buckles until she spotted the little grizzly foreman. He was arguing with a young woman with deep red hair and light brown eyes that crackled with anger. Her smooth round hips were poured incredibly tightly into a pair of denims. Repeatedly, she was smacking her white hat against her knees as she directed a barrage of curses and indistinguishable insults at the red-faced litle man.

"I'm gonna bend you over my knee, little lady. If your ma knew you were cussing like that, you'd have lye soap for dinner." With a jerk of his head, Freddy spat a stream of tobacco juice onto the ground.

"You sawed-off tree stump. I don't give a hoot what you say. We're going to the street dance. I've been planning it all year and I'm not going to let a stupid litle bump on the head stop me now."

"You just go on and find somebody else to take you to the street stomping. Red, and let Jesse go to the hospital like he should."

"Don't call me Red!" she screamed. Several heads turned toward her, then shook knowingly and chuckled.

"Don't you have any feelings at all, gal? Jesse's hurt."

"Oh, shoot. He's been kicked in the head before."

The short man removed his straw hat, ran his fingers through his sandy hair, then crammed the hat back on, hissing the air between clenched teeth.

"Looky. There must be at least half a dozen fellas hanging 'round here that'd be proud to take you to the galderned dance, Bonnie Sue. You just go on with one of 'em and I'll explain to your ma."

"I don't want to go with any of those goat ropers. I want Jesse." She swirled, sending the sleek pageboy twirling around her neck as she stomped away.

Marlene, feeling the heat radiating from her cheeks, stepped up to the foreman and tapped him on the shoulder.

"Freddy?"

He jumped. "Huh!" Oh, sugar lamb, it's you. You look like a half-drowned rat." His knowing old eyes gave her rain-soaked form a rapid sweep.

Marlene's gaze dropped to the green jersey dress, now plastered around her body in a limp gray sheath, revealing the outline of her bra and emphasizing the rapid rise and fall of her breasts as she tried to bring her breathing under control.

"How's Jesse?" she asked, pressing her purse to her chest. "Freddy,' she repeated firmly when he remained silent, "you wouldn't be trying to hide anything from me, would you? Is he really all right?"

The short man lowered his head and removed his hat, holding it tightly in his hands and fidgeting with the brim.

"He got hit in the head. Just a graze looks like, but ... well, you never can be too sure with a head bump. Maybe it knocked some sense into his fool noggin. He oughta leave old Texas Twister to the younguns, you know." He shook his head sadly, clucking his tongue and shoving the tobacco wad to the other cheek.

"Are you taking him to the hospital?"

"Well ..." Freddy shifted his small frame and cast a quick dart in the direction that the redhead had vanished. "I'm sure as hell trying to, sugar dumpling. But that fool gal – " He spat fast and hard. "She's trying to convince him to go the street dance down by the courthouse. Even if that bump ain't serious, he's sure as shooting gonna be one sore sonofa ... uh ... one sore fella. Top and bottom." He chuckled, but the sound didn't go well with his worried gray eyes. How well Marlene

53

remembered the many times Jesse would limp after a throw, and ease in and out of the old pickup with gritted teeth, never complaining, pretending it didn't hurt when she ran her fingers over cracked ribs, or dislocated joints, or busted and bruised cheeks. And the fever that permeated his body only served to make him all the more desirable.

"Freddy?" She paused, dropping her eyelashes. "Who is that redhead?"

"Why, you know her, honey. That's Bonnie Sue. Mrs. Yancy's youngest. She's the only one left home now. She goes to the university but comes back during the summers." He let out a controlled sigh.

"Oh, yes, Bonnie Sue." Marlene formed the mental picture of a teenager with a splattering of freckles over a turned-up nose and shiny braces.

"Come on, sugar lump, I've got me an idea." Freddy shoved his hat back on and grabbed her hand, leading her through the milling cowhands who were bustling about, pulling horses into trailers or stalls, throwing in feed, and some brushing down the animals for the night. Marlene followed reluctantly, unsure of what he was up to, and at the sight of the tall dark-haired man sitting on a bench, pressing his head to the sweaty concrete wall, her heart rolled over. She almost didn't see the redhead who was walking up to Jesse, handing him a cold Coke. His eyes were tightly closed, and apparently he didn't hear the girl, for she pushed the cold can against his cheek to get his attention and he jumped. The sight of the dark eyes flying open sent an electrifying charge down Marlene's body, and her fingers began trembling uncontrollably.

"Freddy ... I – I can't." She tried to turn in her tracks, a sense of helplessness and petrification seizing her.

"Hush up, gal. Come on. We're gonna get that stubborn mule to the hospital by hook or crook. Hey, Jesse, boy, looky here who I found wandering 'round the grounds looking like a little lost doggie." He yanked Marlene's arm with a strength that was amazing for such a tiny man, and she stumbled to a halt in front of the seated man, acutely aware that all eyes were plastered to her outrageous slinkly green dress and high heels. At the sound of his name, Jesse jerked his head around and suddenly his lips fell apart and his dark eyes snapped to life. Then as his gaze poured over the wet revealing dress and came to rest on Marlene's own uneasy eyes, the lips grew taut. The tanned fingers that had stopped in midact of opening the Coke can snapped the lever off with a loud pop and hiss. In silence Jesse brought the can to his lips and sipped thoughtfully, his dark eyes still staring at her from over the top of the aluminum can.

"Hello, Jesse, it's good to see you again.' Marlene hated her voice for being so tiny and quivery.

He lifted the can slightly and gave a half-nod, his eyes boring into her face.

"What'd Freddy bribe you with to get you out here?" his icy voice crackled in the air.

Marlene felt a surge of heat rushing to her cheeks, but Freddy stepped closer and spoke up.

"Jesse, boy, you'd best be getting on to the hospital. I can come back and load up the horses later. Is that head of yours about to split wide open?" Freddy knelt beside Jesse and leaned forward, his gnarled old hand gently touching the streak of dried blood that blended with the dark hair. Jesse winced lightly and ducked away from the exploring fingers.

"I'm all right, Freddy. Go ahead and load up now. "Even though he spoke to the squatted man, his eyes never left Marlene's.

"Like hell I will, you stubborn jackass ... uh, 'scuse me." Freddy tipped his hat to Marlene, then threw the redhead a snarl as she moved closer.

"He's all right, you old mother hen. Get on outa here." The redhead slipped next to Jesse on the bench, looping her arm through his and glaring up at Marlene. "Are you that Whitney girl that used to come out to the ranch when I was a kid?" she asked blatantly, her face screwed impishly. Although her freckles had faded and her hair was done in a sleek modern style now, the turned-up nose and pouty lips gave her the look of a fifteen-year-old rather than her actual twenty years. She asked something else, but Marlene didn't hear what it was, for her eyes saw Jesse's face growing paler by the second and the beads of perspiration starting to pop on his forehead. The dark eyes tried to stare her down, but Marlene knew they were struggling just to stay open. Gently pushing Freddy aside, she slipped onto the bench beside Jesse, on the other side of Bonnie Sue.

"Jesse, please, let him take you to the doctor. You look terrible." Her brows were knitted in compassion and she bit her lower lip as she took a closer look at the gash on the side of his head. He turned, his face only inches from hers, and her heart raced. She felt the heat of his feverish body and heard his slightly ragged breath while she studied the face. The eyes had a few more tiny lines derived from six more years of squinting in the unyielding Texas sun, and the tanned skin no longer radiated the dewy freshness of youth. The devilish glint in his dancing brown eyes had been transformed into something hard, like chips of ebony. And the lips that had once easily curled into a wicked irresitible smile now held their firm, taut position, as if it would take much more than the reappearance of an old love to make them relax. Gone was the restless ambitious look of a young man whose dreams and schemes had a kind of desperate all-or-nothing undertone. Before her was a mature man, with eyes that, in spite of the pain in them, emitted confidence and the calm expression of one who has achieved his goals. Though he'd never been a profuse talker, the silence and intensity of his countenance was frightening to Marlene. She was thankful when Freddy put his hand gently on Jesse's knee and said, "come on, son, let's go."

The redhead jerked her head angrily towards the little man.

"No! He promised to take me to the street dance. I've waited all year for him to do it." She squeezed Jesse's arm tight and gave it a rough shake. "You'll be all right, won't ya, honey?" She leaned over and placed a quick kiss on his damp cheek. "Come on." She stood up, taking his arm and trying to force him up.

"Bonnie Sue!" Freddy screamed, grabbing Jesse's other arm and giving it a pull. Jesse moaned and closed his eyes.

"Hold on a minute. I feel like a hunk of saltwater taffy." He yanked his arms away from both sides and opened his weary eyes a slit. "You go on without me, Bonnie. I'll try to join you as soon as the doctor wraps my head. . . . Go on."

The redhead glared at him in sizzling anger for a moment, then threw an ire-dipped dart at Marlene before swirling and stomping out of sight.

"Somebody ought to fan her britches," Freddy mumbled as he eased Jesse up.

Although Freddy was a foot shorter than the dark-eyed man, he wrapped his arms around Jesse's waist and said, "Lean on me, son," as Jesse began wobbling towrd the barn door. Then, doubled over with his load, Freddy turned his head slightly toward Marlene. "Well, come on gal, shake a leg. Give me a hand here."

Marlene stood timidly by, looking at Jesse's sweat-covered face. She felt his dark eyes boring into her as she stepped closer until she was only a foot away. Feeling awkward and out of place, she stood in silence, swallowing hard, unable to force herself to place her arm around his waist for fear of his rejection. A little sigh of impatience escaped from Freddy's lips, and she turned her gaze to the short man. At the same time she felt a slight shifting movement, and before her eyes could lift to meet Jesse's, a warm strong arm slipped across her back and encircled her shoulder. As the fingers clasped into her flesh lightly, cautiously, almost tenderly, a spark ignited within Marlene's heart. The touch, so familiar and yet bearing the excitement of a stranger's hand, burned into her arm.

"I'll owe you one for this," Jesse said softly as their eyes locked and his arm gently forced her closer until her side pressed against his. The pounding of her heart drowned out the sounds of the rodeo, and easing her arm around his waist, feeling the hardness and strength of his body, Marlene knew that it was she, not Jesse, who needed the support.

Chapter Four

The threesome agreed to drive to the hospital in Marlene's car since the pickup was still hitched to the horse trailer. Jesse sat in the front seat for his long legs needed the extra room, and Freddy crawled into the cramped back of the sleek sports car. As Marlene engaged the gears and effortlessly hummed out onto the highway, Jesse's eyes scoured the inside of the car, then came to rest on Marlene's profile with a slight look of disgust. Marlene's first glance to the passenger side caught that and she quickly turned away. The softness of the dark eyes that had glimmered for an instant in the stables when he wrapped his arm around her shoulder, submitting, admitting that he needed her, had suddenly vanished to be replaced by a cold black glint.

"Well, you two ain't jawing much for a couple of old love birds that ain't seen each other in six years." Freddy, chuckling, leaned forward and slapped Jesse's back.

"Some things don't have to be said out loud, Fred," Jesse replied in a forcibly controlled voice. Marlene fought the urge to look at his face again but her heart cowered within her chest, throbbing madly. Freddy seemed to sense the significance of the words, for he cleared his throat and plopped back on the seat. The silence was filling the car to the point of bursting when Marlene spoke out.

"I've forgotten how to get to the hospital. Do I turn on Main?"

"Yes," both men answered simultaneously. It might have been funny at another time and place.

"Mighty pretty car, sugar plum," Freddy said as a new silence began to creep over the two in the front sea. "But those city fellas must be little runts like me. A man like Jess'd get seven years' stunted growth from driving one of these contraptions too long. Must be a cheap little ol' thing." He cracked his knuckles against the inside of the door and twisted his head around, examining the roof. Marlene didn't have the heart to tell him the sports car cost more than his new pickup. She jumped in surprise when Jesse spoke.

"No, Fred, they're not as cheap as they look. This a novelty car, right, Marlene? The kind that doesn't have much function, but looks good sitting in the driveway of a fancy town house in Dallas."

A flash of anger shot through Marlene, and her words were out before she could stop them.

"It's not even my car. She had made the mistake, and it was too late to retract, so she didn't bother waiting for Jesse's inquisition. "It belongs to the editor of the magazine I work for. He likes his reporters to look good when they go on assignments. My car is a little Japanese thing – ugly as sin and cheap, cheap, cheap." She felt a tiny bit proud as she glanced over to see the smug expression lifted from Jesse's face. She heard him suck in air before answering in a calm voice.

"That editor must have a lot of sports cars then. Or else he's only got one reporter." When Marlene made no reply, he spoke again, with more confidence. "Or maybe just one reporter that he cares about, one way or another."

"I know what you're getting at, Jesse, and you're wrong – "

"Hey, hey, sugar lamb, you're gonna

miss your turn," Freddy interrupted, tapping her shoulder. "Right here. Then go on down two blocks to Elm Street. You won't recognize the old hospital, honey. Got two new wings. The town's growing; lots of sick folks nowadays." He chuckled, then plopped back and cut off a hunk of Bull Durham, popped it into his jaw, and began working the stiff piece into a manageable wad. "Park right over there to the left of that big ol' yeller van," he said, his words only half understandable. Marlene gave him a grateful look and parked the car, then remained in the seat, unsure if her legs would support her. But when Freddy, trying to get out of the cramped back seat, began cussing, she had to get out to help him. She gave Freddy her hand and lifted him out of the low-slung car, then saw Jesse striding for the hospital, outstripping them by twenty yards. In spite of his obvious anger at her, she was relieved to see that he could stand on his own feet at least.

"Dern fool boy don't know when to leave well enough alone, does he, gal?"

"He has the right to say or ask anything he wants, Freddy. We have no ties any longer."

"Shoot!" He spat. "You ain't much swifter than he is, mule head." He pinched her arm and began spinning his bowlegs after Jesse. When they arrived inside, Marlene saw Jesse leaning casually against the registration desk, chatting in his easy, friendly way with the nurse. In her early twenties, the girl gazed up into his eyes with adoration, raptly smiling and nodding and listening to his every word. Freddy pushed up to the counter and placed his hat on top of a pile of forms.

"Pardon me, little miss, have you called Dr. Spinks yet?"

"Yes, sir. He'll be here in a few minutes. He was just telling me earlier tonight that he'd be expecting to have to mend a few broken bones for the next week while the rodeo's going on. But we never thought we'd see anyone as famous as Mr. Franklin here." She smiled demurely, glancing up at Jesse from under long blond eyelashes. Marlene felt ill. Was she just seeing things or was every girl in town really trying to seduce Jesse in front of her eyes? What had happened to the morals of the small-town girls – or the sly little innocent games they used to play with boys, leading them on, then backing away, talking just on the

66

brink of enticing subjects but acting shocked and insulted if a boy actually mentioned a suggestive term. She didn't remember being jealous of every girl six years ago. But then, six years ago, she had had no reason to be. She was Jesse's girl, plain and simple. She was faithful to him and he to her. He flirted, of course. Anyone as deliciously handsome as he was had to be tempted. But somehow his little jokes and winks and flashing grin back then only made her proud. It was as if he'd been telling the other girls he was terrific, good-looking, sexy, and totally hers. That was the difference. Now he was all those things except the last. Now he was on the open market up for bid.

A wave of self-disgust swept over Marlene, and she quietly walked into the waiting room and sat on the sofa. She was dreadfully thristy and saw a Coke machine and water fountain at the other side of the room, but her feet refused to budge. She leaned her head back against the cushion, realizing for the first time that she hadn't rested in over eighteen hours. All she'd eaten was the popcorn and peanuts at the rodeo, and a dull throb in her right foot indicated that she must have stepped on something sharp while running to the back stalls. She heard the sound of ice crunching into a Coke cup and a gurgle of liquid, but didn't open her eyes. The slight shake of the couch as a body sat down next to her and the sudden touch of a warm hand forcing her to take the cold paper cup made her eyes fly open.

"You look beat," Jesse said, leaning his head back against the sofa too.

She looked at the Coke cup, then drank half its contents in one draw. "Thanks."

"Marlene..." He paused, turning his head to face her, but still leaving it pressed to the back of the couch. Marlene stared down at the now empty cup, turning it in her fingers absentmindedly. "Marlene, listen. I'm sorry about what I said back there."

She lifted her gaze and examined his expression carefully, judging the sincerity of his words. She was shocked to see how pale and troubled he looked. The perspiration was dripping from his temples and the dark hair stuck to his forehead. A wave of guilt and concern rippled over her.

"Well, you never were one to mince words, Jesse."

"Guess not. And it's gotten me in more

trouble than I care to talk about. But you already know that."

"Yeah, I know." She felt a weak smile touch her lips. "Jess, you look terrible. Is the doctor coming soon?"

"Yes. He's with an emergency – a car wreck. I'm not that bad."

Marlene, instinctively reaching up to push aside the wet hair from his forehead, recoiled at the intense heat her hand met.

"Jess, you're burning up."

Jesse took her hand and brought it to rest against his thigh, where he cradled it in his own hand.

"It's nothing. Don't be such a worrywart."

"And what are you? Always the Spartan? You wouldn't admit you hurt if your life depended on it."

He flashed a grin. "I didn't know you cared."

"Cared?" She swung toward him, her still damp hair falling limply around her neck. "How can you say that? You're the only one I ever did care about. You . . . oh, shoot!" She snatched her hand free from under his and stalked over to the Coke machine. She bought another cup, guzzled it down, then tossed the ice into the

69

trashbin before returning to the couch. As she sat down, she noticed something dark near Jesse's lower ribs that hadn't been there before. He caught her glance and quickly folded his arms so that the spot was covered. With a burst of anger, Marlene jerked his arms down after a struggle and touched the stain. It was wet and, as she raised her finger, she saw the tips were red.

"Oh, Jesse. You got kicked in the side too, didn't you?"

He shrugged.

"Were you even going to tell the doctor?" she demanded.

"Of course I was. But I didn't want you to get hysterical like you used to. Hell, it was always so embarrassing when you'd fuss over me like I was an invalid or something."

"Something is right. A stubborn mule without a lick of sense. Oh, Jesse..." She choked down a sob and felt hot tears blinding her sight.

He shook his head slowly, glancing around the room to see if anyone was watching. "Here we are again. Fighting in the hospital waiting room like a couple of banty roosters. Just like old times, huh?"

"Yeah, just like the good old days." She

withdrew a hankie from her purse and blew her nose.

"I guess you're going to walk out on me again this time, right?" He shifted his weight and an uncontrollable grimace twisted his lips in pain before he could settle his position and regain his composure.

"Seeing you in pain isn't my idea of fun, Jesse. I didn't come here to – "

"Why did you come, anyway?" His words came out terse, through teeth clenched in pain. Before she could reply, he had seized the edge of the couch, his knuckles white from the intensity of his grip; then, with a forward lurch, he collapsed onto the sofa cushions.

"Jesse!" She grabbed his hand and dropped to her knees. Almost simultaneously the glass doors opened and the doctor, a nurse, and Freddy rushed in. The physician knelt down and gently turned Jesse over. He took one look at his face and head wound, then groaned.

"Ah, hell, Jess. When are you going to listen to me? Nurse, go get the stretcher. I wanted to go home early tonight, you old rascal." He gave Jesse's arm a fond rub, then glanced at Marlene's worried face and winked. "We'll take care of him."

Marlene nodded, trying to steady her shaking knees. The stretcher arrived and as the orderly lifted Jesse's body onto it, Marlene felt the hand that was still inside her own squeeze tighter. Jessie was placed on the taut white cloth, and now, feeling the lean, tanned fingers scraping out of her hand, Marlene was consumed with heartache. She quickly leaned over, placing a kiss on the hot cheek, and whispered, "I won't leave you this time, Jesse. I promise." She thought she saw his dark eyelashes flicker against his pale cheek; then he was carried away. After the group had vanished down the hall, with Freddy tagging behind, his straw hat twisting in his hands, Marlene returned to the waiting room for her purse. She sat down on the sofa, and, with a sudden uncontrollable shudder, dropped her head down to her hands and wept.

An hour later Marlene started and sat up, scanning the room in the puzzlement of disorientation. With a sigh, she pushed her tangled hair back and looked up into the kind gray eyes of Freddy.

"I – I must have fallen asleep. How's

Jesse?"

"He's gonna be fine, dumpling. I've gotta get on back to the grounds. I'm riding back with one of Jesse's buddies."

"Sure, I understand. I'll stay here the rest of the night."

"There ain't no need for that. Doc Spinks says he'll be fine after a night's rest. The boy's just been pushing himself so much lately. Doing a hundred things at the same time, going every which way at once. He really had no business riding in that rodeo. This rest will do him good."

"Well ... I'd feel a lot better staying here. Just in case something ... some complications..." She was unable to finish the sentence.

"Naw, you listen here, gal. The doc said Jesse's gonna be just fine. He didn't find a concussion or nary a broken bone. He just wants the boy to rest up tonight. He'll be up and kickin 'round by daybreak." Freddy patted Marlene's head fondly and winked. "Give Mrs. Yancy a call and tell her what happened, then you hustle on out there. She'll be proud to have you for a spell. You ain't planning on staying at that run-down, flea-bitten motel on the highway, I hope. Not with Lupe's good

73

cooking just waiting for your taste buds."

Marlene smiled. Guadalupe certainly was the best cook a ranch could hope for, and the thought of a plate of tantalizing, spicy Mexican food made her mouth water.

"Okay, I'll call Mrs. Yancy. And even if I don't go out there tonight, I guess I'll see you tomorrow. Unless..."

"Now, nothing's gonna happen. Are you addled in the head or something? Do you think I'd go off and leave that boy if I was worried one little bit, you stubborn filly. Why, a body'd think it was you got whacked up the way you're talking." The old man chuckled and shook his head, then gave her hand a squeeze. "Adios, dumpling." He winked again before replacing his straw hat on his head and sauntering out of the waiting room on his spindly legs.

After he had vanished through the swinging glass doors Marlene fished a quarter out of her coin purse and dialed the Yancy Ranch number. The phone rang three times before a woman's voice crackled over the line.

"Mrs. Yancy ... this is Marlene Whitney!"

Soon the two women were talking as if

the last six years of silence had never occurred. Before Marlene realized it, their conversation had turned to the rodeo and Jesse.

"I wish you'd check in on that rascal and make sure he's all right before you come on out here," Mrs. Yancy asked.

Marlene promised to look in on him. She probably would have done so anway.

"But it's not necessary to offer me a place to stay. I can – "

"No buts, little lady. You can stay in Jenny's room. It hasn't been touched since the day she got married. Why, girl, it'll be so good to see your pretty face again. Just like old times – Jesse's girl in the house." She laughed a deep belly laugh that filled the phone booth with its warmth and Marlene felt her cheeks turning hot. "Now, you do like I say and check up on the fool boy, then come on out here. Make the stubborn yahoo sit tight till the doctors tell him he can leave. I'll be expecting you later on tonight. If you don't show, I'll send some of the ranch hands out after you with my double-barrel shotgun." She laughed again and Marlene joined in in spite of herself.

"Okay, Mrs. Yancy, you've convinced

me. I'll see you later."

"Adios."

Wearily, Marlene sought out the receptionist desk. By now the cute blonde had been replaced by a pretty young Mexican girl. Since Marlene was the only other person in the hall, the girl quickly looked upon hearing the tap of high heels on the cold polished floor.

It took all Marlene's sly wit to get the girl to tell her Jesse's room number, for visiting hours were long over. Finally, under the pretext of visiting a nurse she was supposedly an old friend, Marlene was allowed to walk down the hallway toward the wards. Feeling all the while that the hospital security would be tracking her down with a machine gun any moment, she rushed down the corridor to Room 115. After a quick scan up and down the hall, she opened the door gently and slipped inside. The smell of aclohol and medication pierced her nostrils, sending a rapid shiver down her spine and reminding her of the times she had to get polio shots as a small girl. The lights were off and the only illumination came from the open window. The blinds had been drawn up, and the large golden moon hovered within the window's wooden frame like a peeled cantaloupe.

Marlene softly trod across the room and stood beside the bed. The moonlight streamed over her hair, giving it a fine, luminous halo, and the reflections of a neon sign outside bounced off her deep green irises. Slowly she took in the length of Jesse's tall body stretched out on the stark white bed. A quick glance around the room revealed no chairs, so she gently sat on the edge of the bed, trying not to make a noise.

She stared at Jesse's face – the thick lashes pressed against the tanned cheeks and the dark hair curled lightly at the ends and around the white bandage. The bed sheet was pulled up only to his stomach, and the white tunic gaped open at the neck to reveal an expanse of tanned skin and dark chest hairs. The arms protruded from the ill-fitting gown, contrasting vividly against the stark whiteness of the cloth.

Marlene's eyes began to glisten as they moved caressingly down the arms, reliving the thrill of their strength and the warmth of their embrace. Then her gaze drifted to the quiet fingers. They were the first thing she had noticed about him seven years ago as he stared down at her, offering the battered baton. Long, lean, tanned fingers. Capable of arousing the innermost latent desires in her heart.

Following an uncontrollable urge, Marlene glided her hand across the bed until it rested on top of his fingers. Her own fingers gently massaged his knuckles and roved over the back of his hand. Tears filled her eyes as she watched her own hand moving slowly up his arm all the way to the cloth-covered shoulder, then across the exposed chest. Her trembling fingers traced a path down the chest, over the concealed nipple, and down to the firm stomach, hardened by years of back-breaking work and pushing his body to the limits of physical endurance. The hand strolled over the familiar territory, wanting to go farther, hungering for the touch beneath them that was reserved for the most intimate of moments. Suddenly a ripple of desire and uncontrollable excitement shot through her body, making the pulse at her temple leap to life. The unexpected thrill caught her off guard and she quickly withdrew her hand to her side.

"Don't stop now. It's just getting interesting," a male voice spoke calmly, with just a hint of teasing.

"W-were you awake all this time?"

"Of course. Who could sleep with all that simulation going on?"

"I'm sorry."

"Why?"

"Because I – I don't have the right to touch you any more than I have the right to touch a . . . a total stranger."

Jesse shifted his body into a sitting position, shoving the pillow behind his back and grimacing as his head bumped the bed lamp. His dark eyes, half-hidden by the shadows, scoured Marlene's physique with unabashed familiarity, slowly taking in every curve as a connoisseur of wine might gently roll the red liquid in the glass before putting it to his lips.

"You don't seem too surprised to see me here. A couple of hours ago you were dead sure that I was going to desert you forever."

He shrugged and tapped the white patch on the side of his head. "Delirium." He smiled, revealing the dimple in one cheek. "Why did you come back to Waterford, anyhow?" The smile had turned into a cynical mocking expression now, and he crossed his arms on his chest and stared at her.

79

"I told you: business."

"Is that why you were at the rodeo tonight, too? Business?" His voice mocked her, and she felt his searing dark eyes penetrating her.

"I didn't know that *you* would be riding in it, if that's what you mean."

"Oh, really?"

"Yes, really. I don't consider seeing you getting your head busted open my idea of fun." She stood up, but his hand shot out to seize her wrist faster than a viper's strike.

"Just why are you here, then, in this room at two o'clock in the morning?"

Marlene felt the heat rising to her neck and ears as she tried to yank her hand free.

"I promised Mrs. Yancy I'd check in on you ... much to my protest. And, furthermore, it's only midnight."

"Mmm, so you're doing it all for Mrs. Yancy. If you say so."

"Well ... are you all right?"

"Of course. As a matter of fact, if you'll hand me my britches, I'm going to get out of here right now." He released her hand and shoved the bed covers back, swinging his long legs to the cold floor.

"Did the doctors say you could leave

80

tonight?"

"Hell no. Hand me my clothes."

"No."

"All right. Better close your eyes, unless you want to get an eyeful." He smiled as he began to pull the tunic over his head. But a sudden wave of pain stopped him. His eyes squeezed shut, and he gritted his teeth and sank back into the pillow.

"See there. You're not in no condition to go anyplace."

"It's just a little bump."

"I heard it was a concussion."

"Bull."

"All right, all right; I exaggerated a little. But please don't be so stubborn. Lie back down and sleep till morning."

"What and miss the big event of the year?"

When her face didn't register his meaning, he added as he tried to sit again, "The street dance. We used to always take the ribbon, remember? How 'bout it, just for old times' sake?"

"Dance? In your condition? I think I'll call for a straight-jacket," she said, shoving his chest back onto the bed. He fell back, but caught her hands and pulled her down on top of him. With lightning speed, his arms enfolded her slender waist and pressed her weight against his firm body. Her struggles were futile against his strength, and her heart pounded faster at the thought of what he could do. As words of protest started to leave her mouth, his lips caught hers, hot and passionate, sending fiery messages down her body. His arms crushed her closer, then he rolled over on his side, pressing her form into the mattress. His warm lips devoured her smooth cheek, then burned a scorching path down her neck that instinctively extended to receive the precious warmth. His right hand swiftly removed the soft white scarf at her neck, then skillfully began to work at loosening the buttons of her dress. Next, the nimble fingers unhooked her bra, then easily slipped to her breast to cup the soft flesh. The blood roared in Marlene's head and the throbbing pulse in her lower limbs ached with desire to have more of his touch. Her back arched slightly as she moved closer to him, her breasts swelling with the memory of what they once knew.

"Jesse, Jesse, I've missed you so much," she moaned, her lips consuming his face and neck with kisses.

"Is that why you come back so many times to visit me?" he said sarcastically. "Is that why you left me six years ago and nearly drove me insane? Is that why you told me you couldn't marry a dirt-poor rambling cowboy?" His words, forced between clenched teeth, became harsher, and suddenly the pressure on her breast was no longer gentle. She twisted her body to free herself of his grip, but he only squeezed tighter, pressing his weight upon her and forcing her back onto the mattress with animal savageness. Through the white tunic she could feel his aroused male desire, and a flash of panic swept through her. He could easily take her; his strength was many times hers. Once she had prayed and longed for the feel of his hard flesh against hers, and cried herself to sleep at night for it. But now the anger in his voice and the cold glint in his black eyes made it something terrifying.

"Jesse, please, let me go. Don't do anything you'll regret," she pleaded in a thick, husky voice.

"Regret? How could I ever regret anything on earth more than I regret having loved you six years ago. Ah . . . hell." He shoved her aside brutally, then rolled over on his back. "Get out of my bed. That's something I should have told you years ago. But I was too young and stupid."

Marlene sat up, trying to rebutton her dress with trembling fingers. She fumbled for the scarf that lay hidden in the bed folds.

"I said get out, damn you!" he repeated, grabbing her elbow and forcibly pushing her from the bed, until her feet met the floor.

"I'm trying! Believe me, I'm trying!" she hissed. "Where's my scarf?"

He glared a moment, jerked the bed covers back, retrieved the white silk cloth from the far side of the bed, then wadded it up and slammed it into her hands.

"Here. I don't want any reminder of your visit tonight." The moonlight bounced off his hard chiseled features – the lips taut, the jaw granitelike, the eyes turned black and staring straight ahead of him.

"Me either. And I'll tell Mrs. Yancy that you're feeling fine. Back to normal in every way."

"Good," he snapped without blinking. "And I'll tell Bonnie Sue not to worry either. Your accident certainly didn't hurt your libido."

He jerked his head toward her and his lips slackened slightly.

"What've people been telling you about Bonnie Sue?"

"Does anybody have to tell anybody anything when Jesse Franklin has a girl? It's considered public knowledge, as I recall. There's not a single gas station owner or drugstore clerk or anyone in town that knows my first name. It's 'Jesse's girl.' That's all I ever was, a nameless face in a long line of your possessions."

"Cut the dramatics and leave before I throw up." He slid his body back down the headboard until it rested on the pillow, then closed his eyes. "Send in the nurse. I've got a problem that needs taking care of."

Marlene glared, speechless, then in a huff, she turned and left the room, slamming the door behind her.

Chapter Five

The car wheels spat gravel as they squealed out of the hospital parking lot. Passing the street dance, which was in its final throes, Marlene felt a surge of anger sweep over her. She wouldn't be surprised if Jesse did manage to escape and dance the night away in the arms of every pretty girl in town.

She rolled down the window to let the night wind cool her hot face. The rain had left the air clean and filled with the tangy scent of wild grasses and herbs and field flowers. With the miles ticking away, Marlene felt a calm beginning to take over, and she was almost peaceful when she reached the large metal sign that read YANCY RANCH, and near it a statue of a quarter horse with another sign reading HOME OF RENEGADE, QHA WORLD CHAMPION. It was like coming home again, and suddenly Jesse and the night were forgotten as she strained to see something else familiar. But in the darkness she could see nothing except an endless stretch of white fence that dipped and rose with each hill and valley. The moonlight revealed a few cattle grazing in the pastures, but the valuable horses were safely sleeping in the clean white stables that nestled at the top of the nearest hill. The tires bumped over the cattle grate, then sent up a billowy trail of dust that shimmered in the iridescent light as the car sped along the gravel-topped road. When the wheels ground to a halt at the front gate and she had climbed out of the car, a pack of hounds, mostly bird dogs, began yelping about her heels. Soon the porch light snapped on and a woman stood in the door frame holding the screen door ajar with one hand and covering her eyes with the other while she squinted into the headlights.

"Marlene, is that you?" she called out in her loud earthy voice.

"Yes, it's me," Marlene replied.

"Goodness sakes, girl. Come on in." The woman dashed down the steps, her tiny, compact form barely touching the wooden treads.

She wrapped her arms around Marlene and squeezed with a strength that her small physique belied. Her dark hair was cropped very short and streaked with gray. Her lean hips were crammed into skin-tight Levis and her flat bosom hardly protruded from behind her gray work shirt. Her face, tanned like leather and wrinkled from years of squinting, bore no makeup, but a pair of twinkling blue eyes and a large toothy smile enhanced her looks.

"You come on in and get to bed. It's almost one o'clock. What took you so long to get here?"

"I stopped to see Jesse and ... well ... he was awake."

"Ooooh. How is the rascal?"

"He's fine. Don't you worry about him."

The woman squeezed Marlene's arm as she led her into the house. She carried the smaller suitcase while Marlene hoisted the larger one.

"Honey, if I spent my time worrying about Jesse every time he got into trouble, I wouldn't have one minute to myself, now would I?" She laughed – a warm and homey sound.

"I guess not, Mrs. Yancy."

"Well, enough talk about that yahoo. Let's get you to bed," she said. After leading Marlene into the house and up the worn staircase, she stopped before a room

88

and opened a door to reveal a frilly pricilla-curtained bedroom. "You just sleep as late as you want, girl. I know you've had a long rough day. We'll talk till our ears drop off tomorrow."

"I didn't see Sam . . . I mean Mr. Yancy. Is he asleep?" Marlene asked, feeling close and warm for the first time since her arrival. But the sudden change of expression on the older woman's face gave her a shiver. For the first time Marlene could recall the blue eyes dimmed over and the twinkle faded. "Mrs. Yancy? Is something wrong?"

"Didn't you know about Sam, honey?" The voice was trembling.

"N-no."

"He died two years ago. Stroke."

Marlene swallowed hard and felt a flash of hot tears come to her eyes. Impulsively she threw her arms around Mrs. Yancy and let the tears fall for a moment, aware of the small woman's trembling form. But when they parted, Mrs. Yancy's eyes had regained the twinkle and her smile covered her face once more.

"We'll talk all about it tomorrow. 'Night now. Sleep tight." She gave Marlene's arm a squeeze that almost hurt, then closed the door gently behind her.

Marlene removed her shoes slowly, almost too weary to finish the minor task. She thought of the sincere white-haired old man who had been so kind and loving to her. With a deep sense of sadness, she dropped onto the bed and closed her eyes.

The thunder of flapping wings, followed by the screeching bellow of roosters, awakened Marlene with a start. She rolled over slowly, not opening her eyes, and felt the slick jersey dress hiked up on her thighs. A soft moan left her lips as she realized she had collapsed on the bed last night without undressing. She glanced out the window and saw the eastern sky, barely light enough to fade out the low morning star. It would be at least another hour before daylight, she thought, and drew the extra pillow up tight to her chest. She had been dreaming of Jesse – he had taken her in his arms and kissed her in sweet devotion, and they had made love in a field of wildflowers and sweet clover. She closed her eyes and tried to recapture the warmth of the too-real dream, but after tossing and turning for ten minutes, she leaped to her feet with a sigh of exasperation and flipped on the lights.

After unpacking and laying out a pair of jeans and a soft, silky purple blouse, she slipped into her white satin robe and began to search for the bathroom. She knew there was one nearby from her overnight visits with Ginny Yancy. While she stood in the hallway, scanning the long line of closed doors, the sound of clanging pots and pans drifted up from the kitchen, and the tantalizing smell of fresh coffee already permeated every corner of the ranch house.

Marlene tiptoed on the hard oak floors, noticing that their shine and color had worn smooth along the centre of the hall from forty years of children's and guests' footsteps. The first door on her left was dark, so Marlene gently turned the knob. The fragrance of expensive perfume and dusting powder seeped into her nostrils about the same time she saw a bed and the sleeping form in it. She was just pulling the door closed when she caught sight of gleaming trophies lining the walls, and a slight twinge of jealousy shot through her. After all, she reminded herself, the saucy redhead had far more in common with Jesse than she did. Marlene began to imagine them going to rodeos together, sharing the excitement when Bonnie Sue won an event, or his comforting her when she lost.

Deep in thought, Marlene now tried the door on her right, taking care to turn the knob as quietly as possible. The window curtains were drawn back, allowing the first pink rays of sunrise to burst through and land on the empty bed. The smell of boot polish and leather struck Marlene's senses. She saw a small table covered with polish, a can of paste wax, and a bottle of silver cleaner. A strange sensation overtook her as she stood in the doorway, absorbing the masculine scents and knowing instinctively that Jesse was staying in that room. The thought that he might be visiting here had not occurred to her before now. He had told her that he wasn't in town for the rodeo, yet he had been in it. And when she had explained that she would be visiting the Yancy Ranch on business, he hadn't mentioned that he was visiting there too. Confused thoughts began to swirl in Marlene's head as she closed the door and rapidly tried the next one.

"At last," she mumbled after flipping on the light and seeing the bathtub. She gently pushed the old wooden door closed, but its warped and aged edge refused to close all the way. She pushed with all her strength, but to no avail. A tiny crack of space prevented the lock from being fastened. Well, she thought, as she untied the satin robe sash, letting it slink to the floor in a soft whisper, no one would be coming up there at five thirty in the morning – she hoped.

She filled the tub with hot steamy water, but her mind was elsewhere, trying to shift out all the facts she'd come upon so far. But nothing fit. She twisted her long hair up and loosely pinned it, then tested the water with her fingertips. As she sank down into the tub, she came to the only possible conclusion: Jesse didn't want to be around her; he was full of bitterness, and the sooner she got away from the ranch, the better. After all, the magazine assignment was no longer a valid excuse to be here. Somehow, in the quiet of the morning, disturbed by nothing but the distant challenges of roosters and the harsh piercing scream of the peacocks, the thought of a terrific story waved in the face of Vaughn Casstevens seemed far too unreal, and hardly worth the pain that would result from encountering Jesse again. If she was lucky, she'd have breakfast, visit with Mrs. Yancy, and be gone before he even returned from the hospital.

With a sigh of momentary contentment that came from having made plans for the next few hours, she let her weary brain relax and settled deeper into the water, closing her dark eyelashes.

At the sound of boots clomping on the staircase, however, Marlene's eyelids flew open. Her first instinct told her to dash for her robe, but her inner logic convinced her there was nothing to fear. Any decent human being wishing to come inside the bathroom would see the light and knock first. She sat up, waiting as the steps came closer, her shoulders shaking lightly from the early morning chill. The steps receded, and she let out a long sigh, then rapidly climbed out and grabbed the large fluffy yellow towel and began drying herself off.

The sudden thump of the bathroom door made her screech, then swirl, clinging to the damp towel. Her wide startled green eyes met a pair of curious dark brown ones. Jesse's tall frame now blocked the door.

"Don't you ever knock?" she stammered angrily, her shaking fingers clutching the towel closer.

"Never had any need to before," Jesse replied, leaning back on the sturdy porcelain vanity sink, arms crossed, and gently kicking the door closed. He appeared in no hurry to leave, in spite of her obvious discomfort. "I didn't know there was a guest in the house."

"Well, for all you knew, I might have been Bonnie Sue in here."

He nodded. "Yep. You mighta been."

Marlene felt her face turning crimson. She saw his eyes slowly scanning her figure, stopping at the loose fold of towel that hardly reached the top of her thighs and then moving on upward to stop at her fingers clutching the terry cloth over her breasts. She waited for him to give some sign of leaving, but his legs remained casually crossed, and the eyes continued their exploring journey over every inch of exposed flesh until she wanted to scream.

"You are rude, Jesse."

His eyes suddenly flew up to meet hers, and a puzzled expression spread over his face. Then he shrugged and smiled lightly. "Maybe. But it's your own fault for lying to me."

"Lying? . . ." she sputtered in shock.

"You said you would be staying at the Texas Star Motel. How could I have possible known you would be here in my bathroom?"

"Yours?" she asked, her eyes quickly darting to the shimmering satin bathrobe draped over the back of a wooden chair. "How long do you intend to visit Mrs. Yancy, anyway?"

"I'm not visiting her." His dark eyebrows knitted, he came closer to Marlene, intercepting her path to the robe.

"But . . ." Marlene stared at his face, her lips parted slightly in confusion.

"I live here now. Didn't you know that?"

"N-no, I d-didn't." The color rushed from Marlene's face and her right hand quickly reached out so she could steady herself on the towel rack. As she did so, part of the yellow cloth slipped down to reveal half of a smooth, soft breast. The dark eyes leaped to the spot, then raked over the rest of her figure.

"You really didn't know I was living here, did you?" he asked incredulously, his eyes remaining on her creamy smooth shoulders and the voluptuous protrusion.

Marlene merely nodded, aware of her trembling as he pressed even closer, ruining any chance of her retrieving the satin robe. Releasing the towel rack might mean quaking even more, but her fingers had to come to the rescue of the private territory that his dark eyes so voraciously devoured. She lifted her hand to the towel and covered the breast, but suddenly felt his strong fingers on top of hers, gently tugging.

"Jesse . . . no." The words came out in a dry whisper. Her heart began to thunder as his hand tenderly pushed aside the towel and let it fall to the floor. While his eyes roved over her naked body, his hand slipped behind her neck and easily pulled out the hairpin, allowing her silky curls to cascade to her bare shoulders. His tanned fingers, which were a stark contrast against her light skin, massaged her neck, then slowly, caressingly, traced a path over her shoulders and down her chest to come to rest and cup a soft, warm breast.

"I'd forgotten how beautiful your body is, Marlene," he said softly, his eyes following the motion of his exploring hand. Then he quickly glanced at her wide frightened eyes and trembling lips. His larynx moved involuntarily as he forced down a hard knot, and the next moment, in a quick, almost brusque move, he stepped back, grabbed the satin robe, and pushed it into her hands. He gave her body one final searching look, then turned, calling out over his shoulder, "Sorry I infringed on your privacy."

"Jesse . . . wait," she pleaded as she slipped into the cold, slinky robe that snuggled against her breasts, revealing the taut tips.

"I've got things to do," he said, without turning. His icy tone forbade further conversation. "One of the mares broke out this morning. She's carrying Renegade's foal. Tell Jewel I won't be here for breakfast." His hand was on the doorknob before Marlene's voice came back to her.

"Well, then I guess it's good-bye," she said, blinking rapidly to bring his back into focus. Several seconds passed before he turned, his face harsh lines of chiseled rock. She extended her hand for the farewell handshake, knowing her hand was cold and sweaty, but suddenly she no longer cared. She only wanted to get away from this man who could so easily rip her heart into pieces. She forced her eyes to concentrate on his hand rather than his face, waiting for it to reach out and take hers. But it remained at his side until she finally looked up. She thought she saw a flicker of turmoil clouding the hard expression, but whatever it was quickly vanished and was quickly replaced by the usual mocking scowl.

"I thought you said you were staying a couple of days doing some kind of research for that magazine. Another lie?" He shifted his weight and crossed his arms. Marlene slowly lowered her hand.

"I was going to stay, but my editor called and said I didn't have to do the story after all, unless I just really wanted to. That's why I checked out of the motel. I only came here to visit Mrs. Yancy for a while. I'll be leaving later this morning."

"But ..." He paused and Marlene thought she saw the turmoil on his face again, but he rapidly turned and reached for his hat, which still hung loosely where he had placed it, on the hook behind the door. He shoved it down low over his brow, then turned back to her and smiled. "Then I guess it really is good-bye. I wish the circumstances had been ... well ... less uncomfortable for you. I mean, with the accident and everything."

"I don't think it would have mattered,

do you?"

After a long silence, he shrugged. "Nope, guess not." He extended his hand. "Good luck, Marlene. I hope you find what you're looking for, whatever the hell it is."

Marlene felt his fingers close around hers. The warmth of his hand and the confidence of the grip sent a wave of torment through her body. Was this what the great, tender, passionate love of her life had come to – a handshake? Weren't parting lovers supposed to embrace, kiss like Humphrey Bogart and Ingrid Bergman with tear-stained eyes and trembling, but sturdy chins? Suddenly Marlene found herself wishing she had given in to him last night in the hospital bed. Why had she refused, when her body yearned for his touch? Standing here now, wanting to hold him, to kiss him, to whisper her love, yet shaking his hand like that of a minister after a sermon, was just one more stupid mistake to add to the long list of errors she'd made with this man. But she hoped it was the last.

"Thanks, Jesse. And I hope you get whatever it is you want out of life too. Only I think maybe you're a lot closer to it than I am." The image of the redhead, her arms looped through Jesse's, flashed across Marlene's mind. "Good-bye."

Jesse's lips relaxed for an instant and parted slightly as if about to speak, then quickly clamped tight again as he loosened his grip and darted past her, brushing the cool satin robe. Marlene closed her eyes, feeling the soft stream of air swishing past her cheek. The last thing she would ever feel or see about Jesse. A swirl of warm masculine air on her hot face.

Two tears slid silently from underneath her closed eyelids, and she bit her lower lip to keep it from quivering. She could smell the aroma of the sizzling bacon drifting up from the kitchen through the open bathroom door, but her stomach suddenly no longer craved food. Slowly, with heavy feet, Marlene dragged herself back to her bedroom, where she glanced at the clothes laid out on her bed. She knew that the soft expensive silk blouse was a sharp contrast to the Western shirts that Bonnie Sue wore, and that she did not wear her new, designer jeans as tightly as the young redhead wore her Levis. Hers was the outfit of a city woman going to an exclusive country – Western swing club in Dallas. She felt instinctively that Jesse would not approve, but then he would never see the clothes. With a sigh, she dressed and went lightly down the creaky stairs. Voices, intermingled with the distinctive laughter of Mrs. Yancy, floated from the living room.

"Morning, Marlene. Did you sleep all right?" Mrs. Yancy asked merrily as soon as she caught sight of her.

"Yes, thank you." She smiled weakly and nodded to Freddy, who was standing next to Mrs. Yancy. The short foreman's hat was off, and his thin sandy hair was slicked down with water and hair oil. His crisp, clean shirt and string bow tie made him look as if he were going either to a dance or a funeral. "Good morning, Freddy."

"Come on, sugar dumpling, you're gonna miss out on the chow."

"I – I'm not hungry. I think I'll pass up breakfast."

"Whooee, gal. I'm sure not gonna be the one to tell Lupe that you're turning down her fancy food. She's been up all morning hustling up special things just for your ornery hide." He shook his head and Marlene realized what was amiss. His jaw wasn't protruding with the usual wad of tobacco. She smiled, and he took that to be

102

a sign of surrender.

"Ah, good. I knew you'd come to your senses, honey lamb." He seized her elbow and led her into the large sunny kitchen, in which, at the center, was a long table with benches on both sides and chairs at the ends. Windows ran three fourths of the way around the room, and since the house was on top of a hill, the glass gave a panoraamic veiw of the ranch below. Gentle green hills speckled with glistening horses stretched as far as the eye could see, and to the left a clump of buildings, painted clean, crisp white, hovered near the center stables. Behind the stables, portions of the training arena peeped through, and out beyond that, a large racetrack with five metal stalls. Far to the right, almost out of sight, a line of bank willows, bending softly in the wind, indicated the curve of the Brazos River and the end of the Yancy property. Beyond the river, barely distinguishable, black specks marked the cattle ranch of the nearest neighbor.

"Buenos dias, Señorita Marlene." A plump, dark-skinned woman, with her hair pulled back in a hard, tight knot, nodded and smiled when Marlene stepped inside the kitchen.

"*Buenos dias*, Lupe," Marlene replied, giving the woman a warm smile and hug. She complimented her on the array of tantalizing food. Everything had been given a Mexican touch – the eggs rancheros, smothered in a hot sauce, and the lightly sweetened bread, and cinnamon-flavored hot chocolate. Fresh fruits, mostly peaches, plums, and melons, were also heaped on the table. Marlene's appeitte suddenly returned at the sight of the luscious food.

After the meal, Freddy left, and Mrs. Yancy insisted that the two of them move out to the back porch to finish the last cup of coffee. Marlene chose to sit in a porch swing while the older woman pulled up her favorite rocking chair. The peacefulness of the summer morning was almost disturbing in its serenity. The only sounds were the distant buzz of cars on the highway and the loud hum of bees feasting on the bounty of colorful zinnias, phlox, and petunias that sparkled with morning dew. A tall, stately cottonwood cast its shadow across the bare dirt yard, where a flock of fat red hens and smaller black bantams scratched and clucked over the morning's table scraps.

After several seconds of silence,

interrupted only by the rhythmic creak of Mrs. Yancy's rocking chair and the occasional noise of her favorite hound dog snapping at flies, Mrs. Yancy spoke up.

"Well, it's a shame Jesse missed breakfast. That mare's been a real pain in his side ever since she came. That boy works so hard, you know. Don't know what I'd do without him." The old woman shook her head and sipped the hot liquid absentmindedly. "If he hadn't come here after Sam died..." Her words trailed off and she stared blankly at the distant pastures. For the first time her ever-cheerful face looked tired and showed the wrinkles that her blue eyes usually camouflaged. "You know, Jesse gave up his chance to be a World Champion Rodeo finalist. He left the circuit and came right on out as soon as he heard about Sam, and stayed until the end. Took a month out of riding in the circuit and missed out on collecting all those points. And never a single word of complaint all those nights he stayed with Sam at the hospital. Then he paid out his own pocket to help with the burial expenses and..." The woman paused. "... And spent his own money to buy that stud Renegade. You know, the ranch was heading downhill even before Sam passed on. Sam didn't want to admit it, but I knew it. So did Jesse. Everybody told him he was wasting his money buying half ownership in the spread – even me."

"Jesse owns part of this ranch?" Marlene's eyebrows flew up and her cup paused in mid-flight to her lips.

"Yep. Nobody thought he could do it, but that Renegade sure got us on our feet again. Now we've got more customers than we can shake a stick at. And every change and improvement has been because of that mule-headed Jesse, who doesn't know when to quit. That boy can be stubborn when he gets an idea in his head." Mrs. Yancy turned to Marlene and winked, a smile once again on her face. "You just keep that in mind, girl. Like right now he's got it in his head that you deserted him six years ago, that you chose the city life over living with him."

"But that's not true – "

"I know, I know. But Jesse don't always let the facts get in his way, if you get my drift. Sometimes a fella's heart is jumping so loud, he can't hear the explanation being given. Now, you just give him a little time. I know it'll be all right." She reached over

106

and patted Marlene's hand.

"Well, time is one thing I don't have. As a matter of fact, Jesse and I said good-bye this morning. I doubt that I'll ever see him again."

"What are you talking about, girl? You ain't planning on leaving this morning? What about all that research you're supposed to do?"

"The story was canceled, more or less. I'm just here to visit you. But I have to be back to work Monday, so I can't stay much longer."

"Here now, I won't have that. No siree. Why, tomorrow is my gal Bonnie Sue's birthday, and we're having a big barbecue to celebrate. My baby's twenty. Can you believe it?"

"Actually, no." Marlene, trying to hide the emotion in her voice, quickly rose from the porch swing. "I'm sorry but – "

"No, I told you I won't hear of it. You're gonna stay for the get-together and that's that. No more arguing. Now, I hope I don't have to get Freddy to hog-tie you and pull the plugs outa that fancy little car of yours."

"It's my boss's car."

"Ooooh." Mrs. Yancy raised an eyebrow

107

and winked. "I see."

Marlene rolled her eyes and started to explain, but felt a sudden wave of exhaustion at the thought of trying to explain Vaughn Casstevens.

"All right. I'll stay for the barbecue, but I have to leave right after it's over."

"Okay. It won't last too long; the rest of us have to work too, you know." She rose and encircled Marlene's waist as they walked to the kitchen door. "I've got a bunch of chores to do in town today. Why don't you get Freddy to saddle up Lady Lucy and ride around the spread? It'll do you good to relax for a while. Take all the pictures you want, just in case you decide to do that story after all. Lunch is around noon." The old woman patted Marlene's arm, placed a kiss on her cheek, and left.

Marlene followed the flagstone path down the hillside to the largest stable. The long, narrow building stood out in sharp contrast against the deep blue sky. Tiny streamers of straw peeked out of the upper half of the building, where sparrows darted in and out, their sharp chirps mingling with the soulful singing of a stable boy at the opposite end. The horses had already been exercised for the day and now eagerly munched on their first meal. A radio sitting on a shelf played soft easy-listening music designed to soothe the animals.

As Marlene's boots sank into the soft freshly raked sandy earth of the stables, beautiful horse heads popped over the tops of the stalls, each eagerly awaiting a pat to the nose. She stopped to pet each animal, admiring the graceful lines, noting the care taken to insure that each stall was clean and the horses well-groomed. She saw several grooming kits with hoof polish, curry combs, and towels lining the walls, as well as some bridles and other riding tackle.

When she came to the stall marked Lady Lucy, she stopped and patted the lovely black neck. The mare, like the other horses, wore a simple leather halter with a brass name plate on the side.

The stable boy and Freddy were nearby, and, on catching sight of Marlene, let out a soft whistle of admiration. Freddy quickly joined Marlene, saddled the mare carefully, then handed the reins to her.

"You need some company? I can get one of these no-count layabouts to go with you, if you do," Freddy offered.

"No, thanks, I think I remember all the roads. Besides, I'm sure Lady Lucy here knows the way home if I get lost."

The old man chuckled and slapped the mare's rump. Marlene had only to tap her sides and they were off, riding at a canter.

Riding along, absorbing the countryside and the fresh morning air, Marlene felt a deep sense of calm begin to flow through her veins. At first the total silence had been unnerving to someone grown used to the hustle and noise of a large city like Dallas, but soon it became a joy so thrilling that Marlene could not help smiling. The gentle rhythm beneath her legs traveled up her body, rocking her into a trance while the scenery leaped to life before her eyes.

It was all as glorious as the day she'd left. And as familiar. For hillsides specked with horses, or red and white sad-faced Herefords, never changed. Gentle hills of green, spotted with spreading massive live oaks or groves of gnarled mesquite draped with clumps of mistletoe, kept their air of eternal peace. Even the entry gates along the highway brandishing signs for the ranches – Bar Double T, Singing Hills, Circle W – stayed the same. The fields echoed with the songs of grasshoppers below and locusts high in trees, while rabbits awaited the cool evening to hop from their holes. Only the fresh white stripes on oily black asphalt and the remains of run-over possums and armadillos served as a reminder that a new interstate highway now split the county where once a simple brick road lay.

Marlene pulled the mare to a stop on top of a hill and watched the distant black ribbon that marked the new highway. She could make out tiny specks of color buzzing along in eerie silence like ants on a tree limb, going and coming with dedicated speed, determined to get where they were going as fast as possible. How removed and insignificant the city life, with its condominiums and traffic loops and high-rise office buildings, seemed now. Her job, the only important thing in her life, was no more than one blade of grass in the immense pastures stretching out below.

"I feel so free," Marlene said out loud as she clucked the mare down the hill and headed in the direction of the Brazos River about two miles away. It had been six years since she had stopped at the river, though many times she had bounced over the giant silver metalworks that bridged the sandy waters in various parts of the state. But never to stop, never to feel the sand sinking under her toes, or the tiny nipping minnows in the dirty green waters. Never to run and splash and laugh in the shallow eddies or build ridiculous castles and sand people on the banks. Never to lie in love, snuggled warm and secure in Jesse's arms underneath the bright Texas stars.

Suddenly Marlene realized that the mare had stopped, her ears pricked into spear points as she whinnied softly. In front of her, about fifty yards off, was the line of swishing, bending willows that signified the riverbank, though the waters themselves were out of sight. Marlene turned in the direction at which the mare was focusing her attention, but saw nothing. She steered the mare to the top of the bank, dismounted, and tied her reins to a willow branch. She saw a deep path that led down the sandy bank, trenched out by thousands of cattle hooves over the years. Wild nettles and grass burrs brushed against her jeans as she clumsily worked her way down the trail. The horse neighed again, and Marlene quickly turned to the right. She saw a flash of color, then heard a voice. Something inside her panicked, but her feet refused to flee. Instead, she softly crept closer and leaned over, then pushed aside a clump of thistle.

A gasp left her lips before she could stop it, and the tall dark-haired man kneeling beside the neighing horse turned in her direction. His dark eyes stared in shock for a moment, then he stood up to reveal arms covered up to the elbows in mud.

"Well, you're not exactly the kind of help I was hoping for, but I guess you'll do," Jesse said, motioning Marlene over. "Come on down."

Chapter Six

Marlene crossed the rough terrain until she stood beside the mud-splattered man. Below them was the pregnant mare, her body buried up to the belly in thick black mud. Marlene shook her head and reached out to touch the frightened animal's forehead.

"What happened?"

"Oh, that big rain we had last night made a mud trap right here. And this fool decided she'd rather taste river water than our good old well water." He stroked the mare's weary head and spoke soft encouraging words to her as he knelt down and began placing a rope under her stomach and around her back. By the time he straightened up, his jeans had become streaked with shiny black mud from the knees down. He took his gloves off and handed them to Marlene.

"Here, Put these on or you'll get blisters. I don't think we'll be able to get her out this way, but let's give it a try."

Marlene glanced at the muddy gloves, then quickly put them on, feeling the warmth of Jesse's fingers still clinging to the insides of the leather. She wrapped her hand around the rope like Jesse, then, on his command, heaved with all her strength. The horse neighed and squealed in terror as she struggled to get free, and Marlene felt the weight of solid horse flesh yanking at the taut rope.

Suddenly, the slippery earth slid from under Marlene's boots and with a scream she crashed into the side of the bank. Like an otter sliding into the ocean, she scooted down the bank on her back until her feet had plopped into the edge of the river. She tried to stand, but lost her footing and slapped stomach first into the mud hole beside the mare. With a yell of pure horror, she grabbed the horse's neck while Jesse stood by doubled over in laughter. She felt her face turning red, but knew he couldn't see it through the layer of mud.

"It's not funny," she said in a serious a voice as possible, but soon her own laughter coursed through her body until she couldn't even hold on to the horse any longer. She was feeling herself slipping again when a long, strong arm reached over and grabbed her and yanked her from the hole up to solid, sandy soil. With her arms outstretched, Marlene stood, grimacing at the sticky wetness creeping down her back. Jesse held tight to her arm until he was sure she could stand.

"I'm sorry. I didn't mean to laugh, but..." Jesse tried to apologize, but another wave of laughter seized him as he looked at Marlene's mud-covered face. He turned her around, surveying the damage, then with a quick move reached down and scraped the mud off the back side of her jeans.

"What are you doing?" she demanded as she felt the strong push against her hips.

"Well, just uncovering the brand name. Gotta keep the designer's name in sight at all times, don't we?" he teased. Marlene snapped her arm free, but he grabbed it again and drew her close. The mud on her blouse smeared onto his chest as he smothered her breasts against him and his arms slipped around her back, refusing to let her go. Looking into his dark penetrating eyes, she felt her heart pounding until she thought it would burst, but then suddenly he flashed a white grin and released her.

"I'd kiss you if you weren't so dirty," he said with a wink and quickly reached for the rope. Before Marlene could protest, he shoved the rope into her hands. "We'll have to use the pickup. Stay here a minute and talk to the mare. Poor thing's scared out of her head."

Marlene stared at the lariat in her hands, then watched Jesse's lean, muscular legs effortlessly climbing up the steep bank. She absentmindedly spoke to the mare in a soft, soothing voice until he returned in a few moments. He paused in front of her, his eyes full of what she almost thought could have been interpreted as affection, then took the rope from her hands and attached it to the one he had hooked to the truck.

"Okay. Now you go up there and back up real slow. I mean barely move, and if I yell, stop. Got it?"

"Okay. Marlene started up the bank, clumsily trying to get her mud-caked boots to take a firm hold. Suddenly she felt hands giving her a boost from behind until she reached the top of the bank.

After several tries she got the pickup started, then slowly backed up. The wheels spun as the mare's weight jerked the rope tight and the squealing animal's legs fought for firm earth. With Jesse's help and urgings, the mare finally caught a piece of solid ground and pulled her body free. She stood with trembling legs while Jesse stroked her mud-covered neck and affectionately patted her and examined her belly and hindquarters.

"Is she all right?" Marlene asked in a ragged voice after jogging down the steep path.

"I think so. She seems very weak. But I know she was only here about an hour at the most. I'm going to let her rest a little while before taking her back. She doesn't look right in the eyes either." He snapped the lead rope to her halter, then gently coaxed her up the bank. After tying her to the pickup, he turned to Marlene, a soft, warm glimmer in his dark eyes.

"Thanks, Marlene. I couldn' have done it without you. I was going to have to go all the way back to the ranch for Freddy. You always were a real Spartan when it came to pitching in." He firmly grasped her shoulders with his hands, then kissed her tenderly on the lips.

Marlene closed her eyes, fighting the moan that demanded to rise from her throat. The kiss was over before she knew it and she blinked to regain her composure.

"Think nothing of it. I wanted to see what it was like to work on a ranch. Now I know," she said with a sheepish smile as she extended her mud-covered arms.

Jesse chuckled, then slipped his arm around her waist and led her back down the trail

"What we need is a quick dip in the old Brazos," he said. He sat down on an ancient gray rock and began removing his boots. "Here. Sit down and take your boots off." He patted the damp rock near him. Marlene glanced at the river, then down at her muddy clothes. With a sigh, she sat down and began working on her boots.

"The next thing you know, you'll be telling me to take my clothes off," she mocked, casting a quick glance at his face. She saw a wicked smile slip over his lips.

"Not a bad idea," he said teasingly as he tossed his boots aside, rapidly unfastened his shirt buttons, and jerked the shirt free from the Levis. Marlene's eyes became fixed on the trim, muscular chest, tanned from long summer days of working beneath the sweltering sun, the muscles hardened from countless hours of back-breaking work – baling hay, chasing frisky horses,

119

swinging heavy saddles, mending fences, chores as endless as the grains of sand on the pale beach underneath her bare feet. Her eyes devoured every taut ripple of Jesse's body as he stood on the old gray rock, poised for a dive. He let out a piercing Rebel yell, then dived head first into the deepest part of the soft green waters, disappearing for several seconds, then popping up ten yards away shaking his wet hair like a dog in the rain.

"Come on in. It's perfect," he shouted at Marlene, who was standing reluctantly on the bank. After a few mumbles and another look at her mud-caked clothes, she snatched his shirt and gingerly stepped into the water. The cool liquid sent a chill up her legs, but as she waded deeper and began splashing water on her blouse, a refreshing sensation soothed her body. After the mud had melted away from her own clothes, she scrubbed Jesse's shirt. By the time she was in water deep enough to swim, she was clean. She swam as gracefully as possible, considering that she still had on all the clothes, then turned to paddle back. Suddenly a hand seized her waist.

"You missed a spot," Jesse said softly,

his hand pushing her hair back from her face and removing a trace of mud. His velvet-soft eyes peered into hers, then his lips caught hers, stifling her breath. The kiss lingered on and on. The strong arms clenched tighter, and his lips showered soft kisses on her cheeks. Soon his tongue playfuly lapped away the beads of river water from her temples, and his words floated tenderly into her ears.

"I thought you said you were leaving right away." His voice betrayed a slight hint of pride beneath the innocent question.

"I was, but – "

"What made you change your mind?" he asked, his lips brushing hers again, then lightly caressing her neck while his hands gently massaged her back, drawing her ever closer.

"Never mind, Jesse. It doesn't really matter, does it?" she said in an emotion-filled husky voice. Her hands glided to his back and felt the bare, firm muscles slick with water.

"Tell me anyway," he urged.

"I – well..." She cleared the catch in her throat. "Uh, Mrs. Yancy talked me into staying for Bonny Sue's birthday party. She insisted I stay till tomorrow night. I didn't want to disappoint her."

Once the words had left her mouth, the hands on her back stopped moving, then released their grip.

"Oh, I see." Jesse's icy voice sent a shiver down her spine. She watched him back up, then, without another word, take his shirt from her and wade out of the river where he picked up his boots and started up the trail. Marlene stared at him in confusion, her lips parted and her wide green eyes unblinking. The throbbing pulse at her temples raged out of control. When she tried to move, her legs felt weak.

After reaching the top of the bank, Jesse turned and glared down.

"Well? You going to stay in the river all day?"

Marlene tried to force a smile, but failed miserably. She began to drag through the waters, making loud swishes and gurgles. She felt the sand tugging at her toes and the layer of dry dirt clinging to the bottoms of her feet as she stepped onto land. After fumbling for her boots, she staggered up the path, her jeans squeaking and squishing out water with every swing of her hips. The dry, hot summer breeze felt good on her shivering body as she walked up to the pickup. Halting a few steps from Jesse, she watched him swiftly and skillfully coil the rope and toss it in the pickup bed.

"Where's your horse?" he asked her after he had finished and was leaning casually on the truck's back fender.

"O-over there," she said through chattering teeth, pointing up the hill.

"Why don't you ride back in the pickup?" He folded his arms and let his eyes rest on her blouse. Marlene glanced down to see her tense nipples protruding and the form of her breasts clearly outlined through the wet silk. She crossed her arms and shook her head.

"N-no thanks. I'll ride back. Maybe the sun and wind will dry me off by the time I reach the ranch." She smiled shyly, then raised a hand to wave good-bye and turned to go. She had walked only a few steps before she felt Jesse's arm close around her shoulder. He forced her back to the truck.

"You're shivering, you idiot. If you don't get out of those wet clothes, you'll catch pneumonia. Wait a minute. I think I've got some old clothes in the pickup." He opened the cab and shuffled through a pile of bridles, ropes, broken horseshoes, and worn gloves and wire cutters. With an exclamation of victory, he pulled out a pair of old faded denims with torn knees and a faded flannel hunter's shirt. "Here, this ought to cover you decently," he mocked, tossing the shirt to her. "I'll take the pants."

Marlene stood for a moment, hugging the shirt to her bosom, watching Jesse walk to the other side of the pickup. She heard the slosh of wet clothes, then the brush of dry denim as it stretched over his legs, followed by a smooth metallic zipping sound. Watching him return, she could not take her eyes off the firm, tanned muscles that rippled with the ease of a stalking cat. Her gaze traveled down his chest to the dark line of hairs on his flat, hard stomach that disappeared into the worn, sensually tight-fitting jeans. Then she saw the jagged cut in the shape of a horseshoe under his left ribs.

"What happened to your bandage?" she asked.

"I don't like bandages," he almost snapped at her. "Well, are you just going to stand there and shiver your life away? Go ahead and put on the shirt." Seeing Marlene glance around for a clump of bushes, he added, "Don't worry, I won't look. See?" He turned his back and pressed his face to the pickup cab. "Go ahead."

Marlene quickly undressed and slipped into the shirt. It was so large that its tails came past her thighs and the sleeves tumbled far beyond her slender fingers. She buttoned it rapidly, and as she straightened up, saw a pair of dark eyes scouring her legs. She rolled the sleeves up to the elbow, then began wringing out the wet clothes.

"You know I can't go back dressed like this," she said as she spread the silky shirt and designer jeans out across the lowest branch of a bank willow.

"No, but in this heat it won't take long for our clothes to dry. Besides, I have to stay here for a while to let the mare rest, remember?" He put his hand on her back and steered her to the shade of a massive gnarled oak about twenty yards from the river. Bumblebees hummed on the nearby thistles and the grasshoppers chirped a lazy, sleepy song into their ears. A small patch of bright gold brown-eyed Susans seemed to erupt out of the continuous stretch of green pastures.

Marlene sat on the clump of grass at the

tree base, trying to keep her eyes off the tight faded Levis that pressed against Jesse's legs and thighs. But the alternative, looking at his bared chest and rippling arms, was even less endurable. With a little moan and a deep sigh, she closed her eyes and leaned back against the tree trunk, letting the warm air gently ruffle her sun-streaked hair. She wondered just how horrible she looked with no makeup or even lipstick on and the clumsy ill-fitting shirt.

"Why'd you have to be so damned beautiful?" The male voice jarred Marlene's thoughts. She quickly opened her eyes to see Jesse's head twisted toward her, his eyes moving slowly down her body.

"I could say the same thing about you," she said softly.

He lifted his hand and tenderly placed the back of his fingers to her cheek, softly stroking the smooth, creamy skin.

"I loved you so much," he said, his eyes scanning her face with deep concentration.

Marlene closed her eyes and swallowed hard at the words spoken in the past tense.

"But not enough to give up the rodeo life."

"I didn't see any reason why I couldn't

have both. It was you that made the decision to leave."

"How can you say that?" Marlene sat up, putting her hands around her knees, turning her face to him. Her long hair, still damp, swung down gracefully to frame her features. "I was only nineteen. When my father was transferred to Houston, I had to go with him."

"Your dear father," he snorted and pulled his hand away.

"Don't make fun of him, Jesse. He's dead."

Jesse winced, closed his eyes for a second, then glanced at Marlene.

"Sorry. I guess deep down I really liked him."

"And he liked you too. But he was just as stubborn as you. He offered you that job on an oil derrick in Houston. You could have made more money in a year there than riding the rodeo circuit for three. And without breaking every bone in your body." She laid her palm flat against his stomach, just below the navel, where dark hairs formed an enticing trail.

"Hell, working on an oil derrick is dangerous too. Especially if you haven't done it before. Besides..." He straighted up and scooted closer. "I didn't want to live in Houston. Don't you understand? I loved the rodeo.It was – well, it was the only thing in life I wanted to do, beside maybe owning a horse ranch. I think I would have gone insane doing any other kind of work. Don't you see, Marlene, even if I'd gone to Houston with you and your father, I would have been miserable. You wouldn't have wanted to be around me. Our love would have died a terrible death."

"So, I was supposed to desert my father? He was going through hell after my mother died, you know. He needed me. And besides that, I hated seeing you hurt. You're the one who didn't understand how horrible it was to sit up in the bleachers, never knowing from one night to the next if this would be the horse or bull that finally stomped or gored the life out of you, or paralyzed you from the neck down like that buddy of yours. It was hell, Jesse, hell. I loved you so much, and every pain you suffered hurt me ten times more. I didn't desert *you*, I ran away from the fear."

Jesse stared at her, his eyebrows knitted and his eyes full of confusion. Suddenly he snapped the twig in two that he had been twirling between his fingers and tossed it to

128

the ground.

"Ah, shoot! I'm sick of talking about it. Just forget it. It was all a big mistake anyhow. You never were my type. You hated the rodeo; you couldn't ride a horse worth a hoot; you didn't know one kind of cow from another . . . it was just a physical thing . . ." He turned to see hot tears trickling down her face, and impulsively flung his arms around her waist and pulled her close. A soft groan escaped from deep within her throat as his eager lips took hers, then blazed a trail down her neck as far as the buttons on the shirt allowed. His nimble fingers began unfastening the buttons, but her hand flew up to intercept them.

"No, no, Jesse, no," she pleaded, feeling his hot breath coming closer to her breasts.

"You were like a locoweed. After I tasted your lips, I lost control over my common sense," he whispered, his hands pushing her struggling fingers away from the buttons.

"What will be gained by this?" her trembling lips asked even as they kissed the sides of his lightly perspired cheeks, feeling the prickle of masculine whiskers and sideburns.

"Everything," came his soft reply. His fingers released the last stubborn button and pushed aside the flannel cloth to reveal a firm, smooth breast. His right hand gently cupped it, and he leaned forward to place light kisses on the soft white flesh all the way to the edge of the brown halo.

Marlene felt an uncontrollable ripple of desire and pleasure undulating through her tense body, and the pulsation in the pit of her stomach beat faster and harder. She slipped her arms around his broad back and her hands met rippling tense muscles as he shifted position to push her gently to the green grass. While his lips devoured hers, she felt the firmness of his masculine desire through the faded jeans against her bare thighs. Her hand slid down his back to his waist, then moved to the front of the hard stomach. Her fingers toyed with the dark hairs, then inched over to the Levis's snap. All the while his tongue circled her lips; then it slipped inside to make suggestive plunges into her hungry mouth. Just as he was beginning to pour kissses in a direct path down toward her breasts, the sound of horse hooves thundered down upon them, rumbling the earth and making them sit upright like a bolt. Marlene frantically

130

began rebuttoning the shirt and scrambling to pull down as far as possible over her thighs. Jesse glared at the approaching horse and rider. Soon the dark animal was upon them, spinning to a halt and the redhead on its back jerking the reins viciously.

"Well, well. Hope I'm not interrupting an old reunion or anything," she said haughtily.

"What do you want, Bonnie Sue?" Jesse asked as he rose to his feet. He put his hand on the horse's muzzle.

"Well, just about everybody's out looking for Marlene. We were sure she'd fallen off the horse and broken her neck or something. Besides, it's lunchtime and Lupe's got all sorts of good stuff ready. Ma says for you to get on back right away." She glared at Marlene, though a smile remained plastered on her orange-painted lips. Then she looked over at the mud-caked mare. "What happened?"

"She got stuck in a mud hole. Marlene helped me pull her out. Then we washed our muddy clothes in the river. Any more questions?"

"Mmmm, I see." She threw another glance at Marlene's bare legs, then at

Jesse's uncovered chest. "If you say so."

As the redhead started to jerk the horse around, Jesse grabbed the bridle at the bit and pulled the horse back. "I say so, Bonnie Sue, so just get any other notions out of your head. Savvy?" The girl's hazel-brown eyes glared at the face below her for a long time, before softening. Then a big smile crossed her face.

"Of course, darling. I always believe everything you say. Especially when it comes to women." She threw Marlene another look, in time to see her reaction. Then she smiled again as she saw Marlene climb to her feet, remove the dried clothes from the willow tree, and disappear down the bank.

In a moment Marlene returned fully dressed. She tossed the shirt through the pickup window and walked rapidly past Jesse and Bonnie Sue.

"See you at the lunch table," the redhead called out merrily, and began dismounting. "I think I'll ride back with you. We've got so much to talk about," she said to Jesse in as loud a voice as possible, and Marlene, hearing the words over her shoulder, winced.

Reaching Lady Lucy, Marlene mounted

and swung around just in time to see the pickup slowly moving down the dusty road, the muddy mare following behind, and the redhead's horse beside her. Marlene could make out the red hair through the truck window, and, not to her surprise, it was pressed close to the broad shoulders of the driver.

Chapter Seven

By the time Marlene arrived at the stables, her hair was almost dry, though it hung in straight silky strands, giving her a disheveled look. She was leading Lady Lucy into the dark corridor, waiting for her eyes to adjust to the dim light, when she saw Freddy and Jesse huddled near the pregnant mare, cleaning off the mud. She hesitated, wanting to speak to Jesse, but afraid of his eyes. And afraid that Freddy and the other hands would see in his expression and hers the smoldering desire of incomplete lovemaking. She stared at Jesse's back a moment, now covered with an unbuttoned shirt. She watched his skillful hands examining the mare, firmly, gently probing. She imagined the touch of his long tanned fingers on her own skin, until her breasts began to throb. With a burst of determination, she thrust Lady Lucy's reins into the hands of the nearest stable boy and quietly strolled past the two men.

Luckily no one was near the staircase as she crept up to her room. She surveyed her disastrous condition in the mirror with a weak smile. Though she tried to think only of the pleasure of Jesse's body, and the warmth of his consuming lips, somehow the image of the redhead sitting so close to him on the pickup seat kept flashing through her pleasant reveries. Jesse's words also kept coming back to her: "You've never loved the rodeo, you can't ride, you don't know one cow from another ... we were never matched ... it was just a physical thing...." A physical thing. Could it be true for Jesse? She knew it wasn't true for herself. She had loved him with every fiber of her being. Surely he knew that their relationship meant more than physical attraction to her. But what about him? The thought was devastating. Was it possible all this time that all those hot, sizzling embraces and passionate pleas from Jesse's demanding lips were no more than the standard male lust? Was it possible that she meant no more to him than a possible bed partner, that he would have grown tired of her after a few nights' satiation?

"No." A little moan left Marlene's lips as

she sank down on the bed. He would have dumped her after the first few refusals if he hadn't felt anything more than an animal drive. Then even as she was pumping up her hopes, she recalled the hard glint in his eyes and the set jaw – the picture of stubbornness and determination. Hadn't he once told her he always go what he wanted? Maybe she had only been a challenge to him. Perhaps he had been satiating his animal passions elsewhere while she had presented to him the thrill of tantalizing hunt.

Marlene got up to brush her hair. Suddenly her hand stopped raking the silky tangles, and her large green eyes filmed over with tears. She laid the brush down softly, then picked up her purse to retrieve her billfold. Carefully she flipped through the photos encased in clear plastic sheaths until she came to her one and only picture of Jesse. She peered at the devilish grin flashing back at her, the dancing brown eyes that had caught a glint of overhead light in the studio, and the thick dark hair whose unruly hairstyle revealed the age of the photo. The edges of the photo were frayed from her having constantly slid it in and out of the plastic sheath, and the words on the back had smears of different colors of lipstick from years of kisses. After a long pause, she sucked in a deep breath and gritted her teeth.

"All right, Jesse, I'll give you one more chance. Because you're worth it. Maybe that Bonnie Sue means nothing to you and she's just trying to make me jealous. One more chance."

After the words were out, a feeling of relief swept over her, and she laid the picture on the dresser top before rapidly finishing brushing her hair. She bathed and dressed in clean jeans and another softly clinging shirt that exposed her curves in a gentle, gracious fashion.

By the time Marlene arrived at the large formal dining room, the meal had already begun and all eyes lifted to meet her. Feeling the icy glare of Bonnie Sue and the curious, seeking eyes of the others, she smiled and apologized for being late, but gave no explanations. Several eyes shifted to Jesse, who sat opposite Marlene, but the darts he shot back at them kept their lips silent. Only Mrs. Yancy spoke, in her sunny, friendly manner, dismissing Marlene's strange absence with a casual comment, and soon the conversation was buzzing again.

The meal was lavish – a feast of Mexican and American foods combined and altered to form a distinctive Texas flavor. Marlene tried to keep her eyes off Jesse, but they stubbornly refused to obey her, much to her discontentment, because each time she looked in his direction he was speaking to Bonnie Sue or she to him. The redhead whispered and even boldly looped her arm through his, pinching it affectionately. Marlene's appetite faded fast, and she was forced to say she wasn't hungry because of the hard exercise she'd had rescuing the mare. It was partially true. She was sore and weary from the ordeal, though her appetite had been voracious before coming downstairs.

After the meal, Marlene declined an invitation to a game of forty-two with Freddy, and Mrs. Yancy, and Jesse. Her excuse of weariness due to struggling with the mare came to her rescue. Climbing the staircase sent little ripples of pain to her thighs and aching buttocks, which were not used to the long horseback ride she'd had. Even her arms felt stiff. The soft feather mattress suddenly became the only thing she wanted as she removed her boots and sank down into the fluffy comforter. Marlene ran her hand over the colorful cover, smiling when she recalled helping Ginny Yancy do some of the quilting. Ginny had been far better at handicrafts than Marlene, and more home-oriented in every way.

Ginny had been cute – not pretty in a breathtaking way, but still very attractive, with blue eyes and a friendly smile like her mother. Marlene had often wondered why Jesse hadn't preferred Ginny, since they lived on the same ranch, or even one of her other younger sisters. Ginny and Marlene spent many a night giggling on top of the deep feather mattress stuffed and ticked by Ginny's own grandmother. They spoke of boys and love and marriage and Jesse, until Ginny finally convinced Marlene that she thought of Jesse like the brother she had never had and that she wanted him to marry Marlene almost more than she wanted to get married herself.

Marlene closed her eyes and imagined how happy Ginny must be now with a husband and two children. What a contrast there was between sweet, kind Ginny and her youngest sister, Bonnie Sue. Marlene remembered all too clearly now, though it meant nothing to her at the time, how often she had seen little Bonnie Sue clinging to Jesse's arms, climbing on him, punching his ribs, laughing and acting like any girl of fourteen might with an older brother. The braces and freckled nose and flame-red hair had served to make her look even younger and more impish than usual, but there had always been something disturbing in the light hazel-brown eyes – something akin to a cat watching a mouse.

Marlene groaned and rolled over, angry at herself for letting the redhead once again ruin her pleasant memories. She was just beginning to feel the weight of sleep pushing her deeper into oblivion, when a sharp knock sent her eyelids flying open. She sat up and rubbed her eyes, then started to rise from the bed, but the knock came again and she realized it was at the door of the bedroom to her right, not her own door.

Marlene sat up higher, peering at the wall to her right, as if expecting to penetrate its wooden and wallpaper surface. She hadn't heard Jesse go into his room and felt certain the person rapping on his door would have to go away disappointed. The sudden thud of boots on hardwood floors and the soft creak of an opening door caused Marlene to get to her feet. She stepped softly in her bare feet to her door and cracked it open in time to see a flash of red hair and hear a woman's voice.

"Hi, Jesse, you busy?"

"What do you want, Bonnie Sue? I was fixing to change clothes."

"Now that could be interesting, couldn't it? You need some help?"

Marlene's face turned hot and cold. She could see Bonnie Sue's hand reaching inside the door and imagined it toying with Jesse's bared chest.

"Is that really why you came up here?" Jesse asked, a light, teasing tone to his voice.

"Well, actually, I wanted to talk to you about the wedding ring."

At the words Marlene sucked in air and quickly pushed the door closed, afraid that someone had heard her gasp. Her heartbeat increased until she could no longer hear anything being said outside Jesse's door. She only knew that the door had opened wider and Bonnie Sue had vanished inside. With trembling fingers Marlene returned to her bed and lay down, her ears straining to hear the subdued mumblings that came through the walls and drifted in through the opened balcony window. But to no avail. Her heart refused to be silent, and soon tears trickled down the corners of her eyes to form wet stains on the pillowcase.

So, give him one more chance! her brain shouted to her foolish heart. No wonder Jesse refused to talk about Bonnie Sue. They were already talking wedding rings. Marlene's mind flashed back to the dining room at lunch, recalling how the girl's eyes possessively roved over Jesse's handsome features. And her remarks – a jibe here and there indicating that the relationship between the two was more than casual, hinting that after her last year in college the wedding bells would ring – all came back now. No one paid attention to the redhead's words. Obviously she'd said them before, and many times; it was nothing new to the people at the table. And Jesse? He'd conveniently ignored most of the girl's implications, but hadn't seemed embarrassed by her possessiveness. No, the more she thought about it, the more it occurred to Marlene that Jesse seemed to be enjoying the little war of glances and sharp remarks between the two women who wanted him. No wonder he'd dropped her so fast when Bonnie Sue rode up to the river earlier that day. Wouldn't any other man have dismissed the redhead, sent her home, and finished what he'd started with the smoldering, hungry woman in his arms? Not if he was engaged to that redhead. No, he had to prove to her that he wasn't interested in Marlene.

With a sob, Marlene sat up and furiously wiped her eyes.

"Damn the barbecue. I don't have to stay here and take this from Jesse," Marlene muttered. She leaped to her feet and jerked the suitcase and overnight case from the closet shelves. Rapidly she began shoving in her clothes and makeup. She no longer heard the voices next door and didn't know whether the couple had left or were silent for other reasons. She was sure she'd heard the creak of a bedspring. But nothing mattered now – all she wanted was to get away as fast as possible. Somehow Vaughn Casstevens and his town house and Mazatlan tan seemed almost decent and welcome after the ripping her heart had just gone through. At least she knew precisely where she stood with Vaughn.

While Marlene was repairing her tear-stained makeup, a gentle tap sounded at her door. With a deep intake of air, she went over to the door, cracked it hesitantly open, and peered out.

"Are you busy? I thought I heard suitcases slamming around in here." Jesse's concerned face scrutinized her, his dark eyes velvet soft and full of curiosity.

"Maybe you did," she retorted sharply, surprised at the acidity in her tone. Jesse raised one eyebrow and his lips formed a low whistle.

"Chihauhua! The lady's got a bee in her bonnet about something. Want to talk about it?" He leaned against the door frame, crossing his legs and arms and keeping his eyes glued to her face.

"No!" she snapped and started to push the door closed in his face. A tense muscular arm reached out and stopped her with confident ease. Jesse shoved the door the rest of the way open and walked in.

"I didn't invite you in here." Marlene tried to shove the door closed again, but her efforts were inconsequential against his brute strength.

"What the hell's going on? You weren't so anxious to kick me out of your life before lunch. As a matter of fact, I was hoping we

144

could finish up where we left off..." His words trailed off as he caught the crimson anger building in her face.

"Before lunch was an entirely different story. Before lunch was before..." She paused, noticing that his face had taken on an amused expression, like that of a parent watching an angry child throw a temper tantrum, and knowing that the child would have to give in in the end. "Oh, never mind why. I don't owe you any explanations." She swirled around to return to the dresser and was almost there when an arm caught hers and jerked her back savagely.

"No, Marlene, you're going to tell me what's eating your insides, if I have to turn you over my knee."

"Save that kind of antics for your younger lovers. I'm a woman, Jesse, not a girl." She ripped her arm free and watched his face go pale, then flush. The dark eyes had turned to pieces of black, glinting obsidian.

"So that's it. You're jealous of Bonny Sue. Come on, Marlene, don't be ridiculous." His hard eyes softened, he stepped closer and put a hand on her shoulder. She tried to jerk it off, but he held on, then gripped her arm with ungentle pressure.

"Well, tell Bonny Sue you think it's ridiculous and see what happens. Besides, I don't care what goes on here anymore. I'm leaving and getting out of your life as fast as my feet will carry me."

"Marlene, you're ... you're crazy. So unpredictable. One moment you're moaning and begging for me and the next you're like a cold rock."

"Don't avoid the issues ... Bonnie Sue. From what she hints, you're practically married. Not that I care, but is it true?"

"Of course not. She's like a kid sister to me. I like her a lot, but I'd never marry her. She's not my type."

An uncontrollable burst of laughter exploded from Marlene's lips.

"Seems to me I heard those very same words earlier today somewhere. Well, if she's not your type, and I'm not your type, then who is?"

The grip on her arm increased until the circulation almost stopped and a numbness began prickling the spot, but Marlene refused to indicate she was in any pain. Her eyes locked with the fiery black ones above her. Vaguely, she realized that every angry word thrown out at him helped to obliterate

146

any chance of reconciliation forever.

"Just what is it I've done to 'prove' to you I have any intentions of marrying Bonnie Sue? Have I hugged her, or kissed her, or shown any outward affection to her in front of you? Have I laughed and played with and caressed her? Just what is it that has you so hot?" He shook her roughly, and put his other hand on her free arm, drawing her closer. Marlene kept her lips taut, her anger rising with each shove he gave her, until finally her fury erupted.

"All right, I'll tell you. Do the words 'wedding ring' mean anything to you?"

"Wedding ring?"

The truly puzzled look on his face left Marlene speechless for a moment. It was one reaction she wasn't prepared for. Her voice trembled with anger as she continued.

"I heard Bonnie Sue knocking on your door, and I heard her say she wanted to talk about the 'wedding ring.' Explain that, Mr. Franklin." She stared up at him, smugly defiant. The grip on her arms suddenly relaxed and an expression of shock registered on Jesse's face, then his eyes began to sparkle. His smile spread until it became a flashing white grin, and soon he was shaking his head in laughter, and laughter, loud and boistrous, filled the room. He plopped down on the bed and slapped his knees, laughing all the while. Meanwhile Marlene's face had turned red.

"What's so funny?" She finally found the words.

His laughter subsided, and he crossed over to her and attempted to put his hands on her shoulders again, but she jerked away. Her harsh reaction caused sparks to burst from his eyes, and his smile vanished.

"All right, be stubborn," he hissed.

"You haven't explained anything."

"No, and I don't think I will. If you've already got me sentenced and hung without a trial, that's your loss. If you think that I would try to make love to you while my fiancée was in the same house, you certainly have a lower opinion of me than I thought. Maybe it's best you did overhear her conversation and got all riled up. At least now I know how you really feel about me. That I'm a dishonest, womanizing scoundrel. Well, don't worry about me trying to be nice to you again."

He pivoted, his tall frame brushing her silk blouse lightly, and sending what seemed like a blast of air to her face. As he stalked across the room, as lithely as a cat, his boot toes scraped the edge of the suitcase. The rasping sound seemed to snap something inside him, for he suddenly stopped, his back to her, and his fingers clenched into fists while he appeared to struggle with some inner demon. When he turned, his face was pale and his lips taut. In silence he walked back to Marlene, standing so near that his shirt touched her blouse. He glared at her for a moment, then drew in a deep breath and expelled it slowly, as if to regain control of his emotions.

"Marlene..." He paused, hung on the word, then spoke with a burst. "Look, Marlene, there's only one woman in the world that I'm concerned about right now." He paused again, and Marlene knew her knees would go weak if she had to listen to any more. She wanted to run, but something in his beckoning tone told her he was about to spill his heart out, and she felt a reverence that he had chosen her to hear the words. He cleared his throat and continued.

"It's Jewel Yancy. She's like the mother I never had, and Sam was better than any father could have ever been. Jewel's been through hell the past couple of years. You can't begin to imagine what she's gone through. Sure, she seems okay to you now, all smiles and winks. But Sam died a slow, suffering kind of death and Jewel almost went over the deep end. She put up a good show for Sam's sake, but maybe that's why it was so hard on her. She never once let her spirits get down around people, but I saw her at night alone, crying. She'd be embarrassed to heck to know I saw it, so I didn't tell her."

He stared out the window for a moment then continued, "The ranch was in bad debt and it looked like she was going to lose it because of back taxes. The IRS folks hounded her like vicious killer dogs until she was on the verge of selling out.... Think of that: her home, the place where she and Sam lived forty years and raised five children.... Well, things turned out okay, but it was close ... too close."

He paused, then sat on the bed. Feeling a wave of affection and compassion for him, Marlene softly sat down beside him and placed her hand on his knee.

"I – I didn't know, Jesse, I swear I didn't. She never told me about all those things. You know how she is – tough as a bull."

"Yeah, I know. But what I'm leading up to, I guess is, well, she's had a health problem from all the strain. You can't imagine ... I mean, when she was talking to me about you being here. She's crazy about you, Marlene. If you leave now, in a huff, it's going to hurt her feelings terribly. How do you think she'll feel, knowing you left because of a silly fight with me, that you couldn't put aside your personal grudge long enough to stay for that birthday party. Aw, I know she wouldn't complain to you or me or anybody, but it would hurt her. And right now I just don't want her to suffer another time, if I can help it. I was mad at you, I'll admit, and when I was stomping across the floor, I wanted to tell you to get the hell outa here and never come back. But the thought of Jewel ... well, Marlene, I'm asking you with all the kindness and sincerity I can muster. Please stay till tomorrow and don't disappoint Jewel. Don't stay for me, or for you; stay for her." His hands idly fumbling between his knees, he turned and kissed her softly on the cheek.

A shiver of pleasure shot down her spine

at his touch, and her heart pounded faster. She knew that if she didn't get away from his body soon, it would start all over again – the desire, the agony of unsatiated passion. Marlene therefore abruptly moved away from his warm form, but she nodded in silent agreement to his request.

"Thanks." He stood up and hesitated a moment. Then as he saw Marlene backing away, he looked like he was fighting off another wave of emotion, but he just nodded and walked out. Through the opened door, Marlene caught a flash of red hair and knew that Bonnie Sue had been waiting outside the door. She saw the redhead slip her arm through Jesse's prior to their descending the stairs.

"One more day and I can go home," Marlene softly sighed as she closed the door.

Chapter Eight

Sleep didn't come easily to Marlene, though she was sore and tired from the long morning's adventures. Her mind whirled with a thousand thoughts, all centered on Jesse. One moment she would be reveling in the tenderness of his touch under the oak tree, sure of his undying love, and the next moment the laughing redhead would burst the bubble of joy. By the time sleep came and her subconscious overtook her weary mind, only the vision of Jesse, his unbuttoned shirt flapping gently in the wind, his hands caressing her, and his body tense with desire, endured.

A loud knock at the door brought her out of sleep with a jolt. Thoughts of Jesse coming back, apologizing for his rudeness, explaining away the wedding ring conversation, and taking her into his strong arms flooded Marlene's mind. She felt a warmness consuming her body as she struggled to get up and rushed to fling open the bedroom door.

"Sorry to bother you, Marlene," Mrs. Yancy said with a friendly wink. "But you've got a telephone call downstairs."

"A phone call? But who in the world knows I'm here?" She quickly straightened her mussed curls and adjusted her silk scarf at her throat, then descended the stairs in her bare feet. "Did the caller give a name?" she asked as they rounded the corner and walked into the kitchen.

"Nope. Some man. Impatient-sounding dude." Mrs. Yancy chuckled and pointed to the telephone hanging on the wall, with its receiver lying on the counter top. Marlene picked the instrument up cautiously, as if it were alive, and placed the mouthpiece to her lips slowly.

"Yes, this is Marlene Whitney."

"Marlene, this is Vaughn – "

"Vaughn!" she interrupted. "How'd you know I was staying here?"

"I called every motel in town. Then put two and two together and figured you'd be there."

"Well, Mrs. Yancy is a good friend of mine. And since I only have two days, it's a lot more efficient to be here, too. Vaughn, is something wrong?"

"Not exactly. I-I mean, I called to

apologize for hanging up on you yesterday. It was rude and thoughtless. I was acting like a jealous schoolboy."

Marlene pulled up a kitchen bar stool and slowly climbed up on it.

"I didn't expect an apology from you. You weren't all *that* rude. As a matter of fact, I haven't given it another thought." Even as she said the words, a little wave of guilt spread over Marlene. She had intended to call Vaughn back, because she couldn't stand to have unresolved feelings of hostility between her and anyone, especially someone she had to work beside every day. But the rodeo accident, then the mare in the mud – everything kept shoving the task farther and farther back in her mind. How strange that she should forget about Vaughn. Because until yesterday, for the past month all she ever thought about was him and his marriage proposal and what she should do about it.

"Well" – his words interrupted her thoughts. – "I'm glad you don't have any hard feelings. Uh, by the way, how's the story going so far?" Marlene felt the hesitation in his voice and knew instinctively that the topic was a difficult one for him.

"Actually, I haven't had much time to work on it yet. There was an accident. A friend got hurt. Then a horse got stuck in the mud and I helped her out ... lots of things have been happening."

"A horse in the mud? You've got to be kidding." He paused, checked the tone of sarcasm in his voice, then added, "Well, have you run into your old cowboy lover again?"

The words caught her off guard.

"I wish you'd stop calling him that; his name is Jesse Franklin. And yes, I saw him. He's the friend that had the accident. And as a matter of fact, Jesse is co-owner of the Yancy Ranch now. He lives here."

The icy silence on the other end of the line grew until a deep unsettling feeling began to gnaw at Marlene's stomach. Perhaps she shouldn't have told Vaughn about Jesse. After all Vaughn was generous to a fault and treated her very well. It was just that he was always so self-controlled that sometimes she forgot that his feelings could be hurt too. "Vaughn ... are you still there?" she asked anxiously.

"Yes. Then your story about being there just to visit dear old Mrs. Yancy was a lie. You're really there to see Jesse."

"No, no. I didn't even know he owned the ranch much less that he lived here when I came out. I didn't learn that until today after I'd already promised Mrs. Yancy I'd stay. It's her daughter's birthday and they're having a big barbecue. I can't leave yet, even if I decide not to do the story, don't you see?"

"Yes, I see very, very clearly, Marlene. You're the one who's blind if you think that you're staying there just to humor some old lady you haven't seen in six years."

"Vaughn, you're being unfair. You don't know all the facts and I don't have time to explain. But believe me, I'm only here as a favor to a friend. There's nothing between me and Jesse anymore. We tried ... I mean ... well, just believe me, there's nothing."

"I'll keep an open mind, We'll talk about it when you get back tomorrow."

After the good-byes, Marlene stared at the dead receiver for a few seconds before clanking it back into the cradle. She drew in a deep breath, her green eyes scanning the panoramic view out the kitchen window before turning. Out of the corner of her eye she caught movement in the little hall that led to the front door. Then she heard a slight tap of boots on the thin, worn rug that covered the hardwood floor. A sudden dread seized her heart as she rushed to the hallway just in time to see the front door closing with a harsh thud. Dashing down the hall, she jerked open the screen door and saw Jesse's broad back and tall frame striding lithely across the yard toward the training arena. His black hat was crammed low on his brow and his gait was supple and fast, almost as if he were fleeing.

A sickening feeling came over Marlene, making her legs go weak, but she stumbled out the door after him. He had easily gotten way ahead of her, and her heart cowered within her chest as she approached the arena. She finally stopped and leaned against an old gnarled pecan tree loaded with young green fruit. She was just in time to see Jesse disappear into the barn, from which he emerged momentarily leading a frisky two-year-old colt. Her mind raced, trying to convince herself that it was only a coincidence, that Jesse had not overheard her conversation with Vaughn, that he just happened to be leaving the house at the time she hung up. He wasn't the type to sneak about eavesdropping – that was more Bonnie Sue's style.

Marlene pressed closer to the tree for support and watched Jesse skillfully swirl his lariat and toss it so that it landed gracefully around the animal's long, sleek black neck. The rope was quickly tightened and the colt began to run at a powerful gallop while Jesse stood in the center of the high-fenced area, pivoting as the horse made wide circles around him. Jesse drew the rope in tighter and tighter, and the circles became smaller and smaller, until after several minutes the black horse was only a few feet away. With hands both gentle and firm, letting the beast see that he was not going to cause it harm, yet keeping an air of command, Jesse stroked its forehead and glistening neck.

Marlene's eyes clung to the lean, tanned fingers gliding along the animal's neck and shoulders, and her heart was pounding faster with thoughts of how those same fingers could arouse her deepest desires with the slightest touch. Her breasts began to ache with a throbbing longing for those fingers' stroke and the pulsation at her throat vibrated in her ears. After moments of soft urgings, Jesse slipped a hackamore about the colt's head, then quickly flopped a saddle onto its back. The colt bolted as

Jesse cinched the girth, but before it could realize what was happening, Jesse's long legs had swung up and the weight of his body was pressing into his back.

A primitive instinct made the colt throw its head down and begin bucking and writhing its body to rid of this foreign object that had wrapped itself to its form. Marlene felt her heart thundering while she watched the graceful pair rocking through the air. How strangely beautiful the sight was in the silence of the lazy Saturday afternoon far from any roaring crowd or bright lights. Only the sound of hooves smashing into the soft dirt and the heavy breathing of the animal and the slap of leather disturbed the awesome peace. Suddenly, the tension inside Marlene snapped like a taut string, and as tears touched the corners of her eyes, she felt no fear, no worry about Jesse's safety. She saw only beauty, only the grace and the strength of animal and man, enemies and friends at one and the same moment. And she understood for the first time Jesse's undying love for the rodeo, and the pleasure he derived from the feel of the beast beneath his legs. Even when she saw Jesse slipping to one side and then thump

160

to the soft ground, she felt no fear, only a calm realization and confidence that he could not be hurt. He rose to his knees and she could see a white grin flash across his tanned face as he watched the colt, which tossed its head and cracked its mane as it stepped high and lightly around the arena, as if boasting of its victory. And just as she had expected, Jesse simply dusted off his clothes, crammed his hat back on, and remounted the defiant horse.

Watching him reenact the scene, like an actor going through a shot again to obtain perfection, Marlene felt no tension, only a kind of envy. This was Jesse's way of releasing his frustrations, of coping with the world when things went wrong. He submerged himself in his work and cut the world out for the moments he was on top of the bucking horse.

Marlene sighed and slowly turned away and began walking back to the ranch house. She had once used her job the same way, dedicating herself to the work and doing a superb job, even winning a few local awards. But now the job seemed so far away that the future became an indistinguishable blur of confusion. Marriage to Vaughn Casstevens might end

161

her worries about working, but it would not end her emotional turmoil. Maybe having children would.

A pain shot through Marlene at the thought. She and Jesse had talked about raising a family many times. But that was years ago; it was a dream seemingly out of her reach now.

Determined not to wallow in self-pity, Marlene swiftly pushed the thoughts away and glanced at her watch. It would soon be dusk and time for supper. The heat of the day made everyone listless, and even though the ranch house had been modernized over the years to include air-conditioning, the blazing sun still left parts of it unbearably hot. Evening was the time when the residents came to life, sitting out on the screened back porch, playing dominoes or cards or swapping yarns.

Crossing the yard, Marlene heard laughter and voices coming from the other side of the house and tiptoes to the side of the ranch where large pecan trees cast dappled shades. Mrs. Yancy, Bonnie Sue, Freddy, and several hands were busy with preparations for the upcoming barbecue. Long wooden tables and benches worn smooth from years of human contact had been placed under the trees. At another end of the yard, Freddy was setting up horshoe pins while Bonnie Sue supervised the stringing of bare light bulbs in the tree branches.

At the sight of the activities and gaiety, Marlene felt out of place. She had no family of her own now, except an old aunt and some distant cousins. Feeling that she didn't really belong, she decided to return to her room.

She was strolling around the house, keeping under the shade of massive cottonwoods and a sycamore, when she saw the silver sports car in the drive. With a sudden jolt, she remembered that the camera equipment was still in the trunk. The extreme heat might damage the sensitive gear, and since the last thing she needed was a scolding from Vaughn for being careless, she removed the equipment and carried it upstairs to the bedroom. As she laid out the pieces, an idea popped into her head. Why not shoot a few pictures of the ranch now – the hands at work and getting the barbecue going? It might make a good human interest story. And even if Vaughn dismissed the story, she would at least have souvenirs of her visit. The thought of capturing Jesse's beauty and grace on the bucking colt rushed into her mind and she quickly slung the camera strap over her neck and selected a couple of lenses.

She dashed down the stairs and trotted over to the training area. Even before she had gotten there, she knew the place was vacated because of the silence. With a sigh of disappointment she clicked a few shots of the empty arena, the barn, and the stables. Then she caught Mrs. Yancy and the cook in a few comic poses over the barbecue pit. With a total sense of dedication to the job at hand, she even got an excellent candid shot of Bonnie Sue practicing the horseshoe pitching with Freddy. The close-up of Freddy's face captured his intensity and the seriousness with which he took the game. And for all time, she captured the cracks and tobacco-stained edges of his lips by means of the camera, which froze his victorious expression with just one click.

No longer depressed, but instead engrossed in her task, Marlene quickly snapped shots of the ranch: the twisted oak tree to which lightning had given an unbelievably grotesque form; the beautiful mares in the fields and the dancing young colts and fillies that had been born that spring. She took notes as she questioned some of the ranch hands who were sitting around. Some volunteered to pretend to do work for her and got out the saddles and bridles, and one young man even went so far as to saddle up an unbroken horse and perform the breaking-in routine for the camera. He was far too inexperienced to display the kind of grace and skill Jesse possessed, but as he flew through the air the lens snapped away, recording the expression on his face, the angle of his falling body, and the painful spill onto the soft earth. Marlene found herself inwardly complaining for having waited so long to get involved in the story, and also secretly developing a grudge against Vaughn for canceling it. In her heart she knew now that it would be the best article she'd ever written, for her heart as well as her mind would be involved in it. She wished that she'd had the camera that morning as she rode around the spread, and especially would have wanted to capture the scene of Jesse and the mare stuck in the mud. Her mind's eye imagined it all over again – the taut rope, the struggling horse, Jesse's sleeves rolled up to expose hard, knotted muscles. She swallowed as the camera hung limp in her hand.

Then suddenly she asked herself why she was doing this. The story would never get into print. All she would gain would be more tangible items with which to recall the pain of the visit. She saw herself, as Vaughn's wife, sneaking out the faded photos of the ranch and Jesse, and hiding them again.

Marlene checked the frame counter: three shots left on the roll of film. There was no use in letting it go unfinished. She stepped inside the stable and walked in the direction of the mare that she had helped rescue earlier that morning. If nothing else, she could snap a shot of it and label it, so that she would know it was the horse that had got stuck in the mud.

She rounded the corner and noticed that the mare's finely chiseled head didn't pop out of the stall like all the others along the long row. An uneasy feeling began to creep over Marlene and her pace slowed. Coming within a few feet of the stall, she caught a glimpse of dark hair, then heard a man's soft voice. Her throat constricted and her heart leaped when she recognized the voice. She turned to escape before Jesse could see her, but in doing so, the camera thudded against the stall wood and Jesse stood up with a start.

His dark eyes, zeroing in on the camera, expressed curiosity. Then he lifted his gaze to meet Marlene's.

"I-I was just taking some pictures of the ranch house and the guys. Hope you don't mind."

"I thought you said the story was canceled."

"It was. But . . ." She cleared her throat. "But this is sort of personal. For my own scrapbook, I guess you could say." She shrugged and stepped closer, placing her hand on the stall gate, trying to peer over it to see the mare's condition. "How is she?" she asked, trying to change the subject, for Jesse's eyes had taken on a strange darkness when she mentioned what she was doing. After a few seconds of staring at her face, he turned and shook his head slowly.

"Well, it's hard to say. She seems okay physically. But she's acting funny. Kinda listless. Being stuck in the mud a little while shouldn't have caused this kind of reaction. Maybe she ate some bad weeds. Or maybe . . ." Jesse ran his fingers through his thick hair, something she had seldom seen him do and a true sign of worry. "Or ... hell, I don't know what's wrong with her. All I know is she's carrying one of Renegade's foals, and she's a grand champion. That foal, when it's born, will be worth thousands, whether it's a filly or colt. The owner wouldn't appreciate it if anything happened to his mare or her foal."

"You mean this mare isn't yours?" Marlene asked, as she stepped closer. She placed her hand on the beautiful chestnut head to gently push back the creamy white forelock.

"No. She belongs to an oilman from Houston. A gentleman rancher, he calls himself. Owns a spread outside Waco. Anyway, she was bred to Renegade here, then the owner decided to go ahead and leave her for the duration of her pregnancy because of some problems at his ranch. He had to go overseas, and all kinds of complications. Anyhow, he's paying well, so I'm not complaining. But if she gets sick, I'll have to foot the bill." His fingers gently pulled one of the mare's eyelids aside and he shook his head again. "Doesn't look good. I'm going to call the vet first thing in the morning."

Marlene watched his face closely. She sensed that his explanations and concentration on the mare were helping him to avoid looking her in the eye. She thought of the phone conversation with Vaughn and the slamming front door. Her heart told her to ask him if he'd heard her talking, but her mind thought of a thousand excuses why the question was better left unasked. The battle raged fiercely inside her while Jesse shifted his weight and gave her a quick side-glance. There was something in the look that was like that of a little boy afraid to speak to the cute girl sitting next to him in school. Jesse's apparent nervousness and attack of shyness suddenly gave Marlene the courage to speak.

"Jesse?" He remained silent, his hands gripping the top of the stall door. He threw her a quick glance, then looked again toward the mare.

"Yes."

"Did you ... I mean ... You didn't..." She paused, looked down at the freshly raked earth, then sucked in her breath. "Did you happen to hear my telephone conversation a couple of hours ago? I was talking to my editor."

The sudden stiffening of his back and his tightened grip on the wooden gate confirmed her suspicions before he replied.

"I wasn't spying on you, if that's what you mean. I was on my way to the kitchen for a drink of water. I only heard what you said as I got to the door. Then I turned around and left."

"I wasn't insinuating you were spying," she corrected in as friendly a voice as she could muster.

"No? Well, then, was it true? What you said to him?"

"I – I don't know. I mean, what did you hear?"

Jesse suddenly turned to her and said through gritted teeth, "You said, quote: 'I'm only here as a favor to a friend. Jesse means nothing to me anymore.' I'm glad you finally said it. I was a little worried that you might be falling in love with me again. I wouldn't want your poor, suffering heart to go through that hell again, now would I?"

"Jesse. Oh, no, Jesse. I didn't mean it like it sounded. I meant you didn't care about me.... I only said it to keep him from arguing on the phone.... I..."

"You mean you've gotten into the habit

of lying to men. You've really changed from that innocent girl I used to know."

"Jesse, please, wait." She put her hand on his arm, feeling the hard muscles through the cotton shirt. As he lifted his arm to jerk it away, the muscles slid underneath her clinging fingers and sent a thrill through her body. Her fingers clenched tighter, and her other hand flew up to assist. "Wait. Let me explain. I swear I do still care. I do. You must know that. You must." Though husky with emotion, her voice remained determinedly firm. At the same time her deep green eyes scoured his face, praying for a sign that he was relenting.

"I thought you did. Until that phone call. Now..." He paused, staring at a point above her head, no longer trying to release his arm. Then his gaze lowered and locked with hers. "I thought that somehow, in spite of what you said, that you really came to Waterford to see me; that you watched the rodeo to see me; that you came to the ranch to be near me. I even convinced myself, after that episode under the tree, that I still loved you. Hell, I even went so far as to toy with the idea of ..." He stopped, then clamped his jaws tight again. "Never mind. It was all a mistake. I admit it now." He shoved her hands away and stalked down the corridor, ignoring the horse heads and soft whinnies beckoning him. Marlene felt a sting of salty tears in her eyes, then with a burst of love and courage she screamed at the vanishing back.

"Jesse, wait! I do love you! You stubborn mule!" She ran down the stables toward him and grabbed his arms until he swung around to face her. She stared up into his unyielding face, determined to spill her heart out to him and take the consequences. "I still love you, Jesse. I always have and always will. But if you don't love me and don't want me, what can I do? I have to go on living. I can't stay away from other men and become a nun. You have relations with other women.'

"A bunch of nameless faces in one run-down rodeo town after another. And all because I was trying to push your face from my mind. But it didn't work. Every pair of lips, every squirming body, left me cold and emptier than before." A cold bite tinged his words.

"But there's Bonnie Sue now. It's obvious that you and she – "

"What!" His word sliced through her own.

"Well, what about that wedding ring she was talking about? You don't discuss wedding rings with someone you think of as your little sister. And the way she hangs on to you and . . . well, she has the kind of personality you always liked. She rides and ropes, and does all the things I can't, and loves the rodeo and . . ."

The sudden explosion of laughter from Jesse's lips caught Marlene off guard and she stared in surprise and confusion until she felt the heat creeping past her ears and to her cheeks.

"Is that so funny? You didn't think you could hide the truth from me, did you, about preferring Bonnie Sue?" She waited impatiently for his laughter to subside. Abruptly it stopped and he put his hands on her arms and squeezed.

"You let me decide what kind of personality I like. And besides, that wedding ring you're so worried about isn't what you think. It's a long story, but it's not what you think."

"But – "

"I don't have time to explain now. Just believe me. I'm not engaged to Bonnie Sue

173

and have no intention of ever being, unless something very strange or drastic happens to me." He smiled, his dimple deepening as his soft dark eyes caressed her face. He stroked her warm, red cheeks with the back of his fingers while the other hand moved to her shoulder and made small circular motions. "As for being a stubborn mule, I don't think they come much worse that you." He pulled her closer, then leaned down to place a tender kiss on her lips. With a groan, Marlene threw her arms around his neck and drew him closer. His arms slipped from her shoulders to her back, forcing her nearer, so that she felt the rapid pounding of his heart and the surge of male desire pressing against her abdomen. His warm lips devoured her cheeks, then her neck, then burned a path down the V of her shirt as far as the buttons would allow. His heavy, hot breath singed her smooth skin, causing her breasts to tense. She felt the nipples protruding against the silky cloth, hungrily awaiting the pleasures of the past.

Jesse gently pushed her toward an empty stall filled with hay, his lips eagerly finding hers even before their bodies had rolled onto the soft yellow straw. Skilled fingers began unfastening the blouse buttons while the other hand slid along the curve of her hips. Marlene started to reach for his shirt snaps, but as the sides of her blouse fell away and his hand cupped her breast, a soft moan escaped her lips and her fingers forgot their task. Her eyes closed in ecstasy of pleasure as his tongue trailed down her neck, making enticing circles, coming closer and closer to the taut brown pinnacle of her throbbing breast.

With excruciating impatience, she slipped her hand behind his head and pulled him closer, until the lips found their mark and brought her to a higher plane of pleasure. As he lifted his head, the first wave of satiation that filled her body was quickly replaced by an even stronger, pulsating desire. Jesse rose to his knees and, in one savage jerk, unsnapped the buttons on his shirt then dropped down to press his bare chest against her soft, warm breasts. The sensation of his hot, hard masculinity against her made her hands instinctively travel through the curly chest hairs, down the center to the hard stomach, then below to the taut Levis. Jesse shifted his weight, pulling her closer, as if unable to bear her electrifying touch, as if prolonging the moment of pleasure that was to come.

"How did we ever manage not to make love this morning?" Marlene whispered into his ear as his lips explored her shoulder, gently nudging the silky blouse aside.

"It wasn't easy, believe me," he replied with a soft laugh. Then, more seriously, he added, "Marlene, you know, I've had a lot of woman, but they all meant nothing. No one ever came close to moving me the way you do. Was it the same with you? I mean, *is* it . . ." His words trailed off and Marlene knew what was going through his mind. He was subtly asking her if she'd made love to Vaughn Casstevens. She was touched and angered at the same time, but quickly forgave his weakness as his hands began to unbuckle the belt at her stomach.

"Yes, it was the same for me," she whispered. "But I had to learn the hard way that no other man could take your place." She felt his hands slow their motion and he raised his head slightly.

"Oh? You sound as if . . ." He paused, laughing lightly. " . . . as if, well, almost as if you were married or something."

"I was," she replied, softly running her

fingers through his dark hair. The sudden rigidity of his back and the quick separation of their bodies that followed put a look of worry on her face.

"What are you talking about? *You* were married?" Jesse pushed her away, though his hands still held her shoulders firmly.

"I-I thought you knew," she stammered.

"Obviously I don't." He sat up, jerking her up with him.

"I told Mrs. Yancy about it. And I even wrote you a long, long letter begging you to forgive me and make another try of it. I didn't know where to send it, so I just mailed it to Mrs. Yancy and asked her to forward it to you."

"I never got it. And Jewel hasn't mentioned it to me in six years. What else did this supposed letter say?"

"Supposed..." Marlene's words stuck in her throat, then, impelled by the intensity of Jesse's eyes, she continued in a stammering, nervous voice, "After we moved to Houston I thought I'd never see you again. I met a guy, very nice. He was the son of the man who owned the oil company Dad worked for. I met him at a company picnic. He was shy, courteous, and – "

"And rich." Jesse's words cut through her like an icy wind.

"Yes, but that didn't matter to me. It was really more of a handicap than an asset because I was afraid of marrying into a rich family. But he turned out ... well ... very conservative and very dull, actually."

"But plenty respectable. Not like a rodeo rider with no house in the suburbs and dinner reservations at fancy restaurants and ... ah, hell, I should have known you wouldn't wait."

"Wait! Wait for what?" Marlene climbed to her knees.

"Wait for me to make enough money to buy a horse ranch and marry you."

"I can't believe you're saying that. I never heard one word from you after we split up. Not one word, even though I tried so desperately, writing every rodeo in the country, leaving messages for you to call me. And writing that letter begging you to take me back. Mrs. Yancy swore she forwarded it, and I just assumed you didn't want to have anything to do with me."

"I told you, I never got it."

"I cried myself to sleep every night and almost turned into a skeleton. Doctors couldn't help. Finally, Dad forced me to go to college. For two years I didn't want to live. Then I met Lawrence, and he proposed. I didn't think I could ever love him like I loved you, so that's why I tried so desperately to reach you. When I got no reply, I decided I had to go on living and put you out of my life. If it hadn't been for Lawrence, I might have gone insane."

"So I drove you crazy, huh? And what do you think happened to me? You're the one that left me, remember? All I could think of was you, and how my life was over. No future to live for. I drove myself to the brink of destruction. I rode in more rodeos than anyone thought possible, three, four times a day, praying that I'd break my neck every time I went out, hoping for the meanest horses and bulls, talking chances that no sane man would take. I must say one thing, though; it earned me a lot of money. You might say I owe this ranch to you. And I almost won the gold buckle, but..." He stopped, swallowed hard, then rose to his feet. "You know, I've been called a stubborn mule, but when it came to you, I think it was more than being stubborn. It was insanity; stupidity." He laughed lightly as he began to pace in front of her. "I never really gave up on you.

179

Something inside wouldn't let go. Every rodeo I went to, I kept hoping that somehow I'd run into you in the crowd. I pretended you were up there watching me. And I still had plans for us. I never married. I could have; I had lots of offers."

"I'm sure you did," Marlene said softly, her heart aching at his agony, her arms throbbing to hold him close.

"Even after Sam Yancy died and up until a year ago, I still had it in my head that somehow, someway, we'd get back together. I knew you worked for that magazine – Jewel told me. And I read every dadblasted article you wrote, trying to see something between the lines. Hell, what's the use of trying to explain to you? You didn't even care enough about me to wait to get married. You took the first respectable man who offered you a house in the suburbs and a snotty club membership. How could I compete with that? Even if I owned a hundred ranches and was a millionaire, I could never be anything more than a rodeo rider to you." He turned to walk away.

"Jesse, no wait. Listen. Sure I had a nice house and a pool and a poodle and all those things. But I was miserable. I wanted

180

sincerity and honesty and the simple things of life like fresh air and love and children. Lawrence hated children; he hated horses; he hated fresh air. He was sweet, but dull. All he cared about was work and golf. I thought I loved him and could make a successful marriage, but it was a mistake."

"Just how long did this 'mistake' last?" Jesse asked sarcastically, his dark eyes searing into Marlene's.

"Three years," she replied in a dry whisper. "I tried for three years to convince my heart that I really loved him. My wealthy neighbors and acquaintances told me I was so lucky to have such an agreeable man; they told me there was not such thing as 'true love,' that passion could only be found at a bar or in a fling with a tennis instructor. But I didn't want to believe them. I tried to turn my marriage into what I felt yours and mine could have been. But after three years I realized it was a mistake. A mistake made by a young, foolish, and heartbroken girl who was trying to forget the one man she really loved. Can't you forgive me?"

For an answer, Jesse gave her a long agonizing look, then crammed the hat back on his head.

"I don't know, Marlene. I just don't know." His words echoed through the hollow corridor as he stalked out.

Chapter Nine

Sunday morning Marlene awakened to a rooster's piercing screams. She rose slowly, a stiffness still in her calves from climbing the steep riverbanks, and pushed open the balcony door. As she stepped out and leaned on the sturdy white rail, the fresh morning air filled her senses with the sweet fragrance of wet sycamores and dew-covered petunias. On the eastern horizon red and pink fingers reached into the pale sky while the morning star flickered before fading into oblivion. Marlene stood in silence, her green eyes staring at the full moon that grew pale with the approach of dawn, and her silky hair moving gently about her calm, pensive face.

Soon she heard the melodic bugling of hound dogs chasing rabbits from across distant fields and the soft rhythmic thud of horse hooves from the direction of the racetrack. In the dim light she could just make out the black specks moving rapidly down the track, trailed by the sound of creaking leather and the low calls of the exercise boys.

Below, spread out beneath the old pecan trees, she could make out the dark images of picnic tables, benches, and a string of bare lightbulbs hanging from the branches. From the looks of a bundle of wires running from a raised podium to the ranch house, she deduced that a band would be used at the celebration. She wondered what kind of friends Bonnie Sue had invited. The thought of the redhead sent a little shiver through Marlene, making her pull the satin robe tighter to her body. The rattle of pots and pans from the kitchen interrupted her thoughts, and soon the odor of rich coffee began to overshadow the delicate smell of the honeysuckle vine that rambled at the foot of the balcony trellis.

With a sigh, Marlene let got of the hand rail. As she turned to go back into her room, she saw that a light had snapped on in the room to her left. Bonnie Sue was certainly getting an early start, she thought, as she walked on bare feet over the cool white-painted wooden slats. Instinctively, her eyes quickly darted to the dark windows and door to her right. She paused, seeing the unmade bed just inside the room and a very dim light, as if from a closet. Her hand on the balcony doorknob, she heard a light scrape, then saw the dim glow go dark. A warm feeling slowly moved through her body at the thought of Jesse being so close, going through the routine of shaving, and dressing, pulling on his cowboy boots, doing all the little things a man did early in the morning while the sun still slept. How many long nights had she lain awake, dreaming of being his wife, of rising with the roosters on some cozy little farm and preparing his breakfast while he quietly slept. And then watching the sun rise as they chatted about the day's work ahead.

The slam of the bathroom door shattered Marlene's reveries and she went back to her bed and lay back down. She knew Bonnie Sue would be in the bathroom a long time, filling it with the heavy scent of expensive bath oil and dusting powder. Closing her eyes, Marlene began to think of Jesse again, by now downstairs sipping his first cup of coffee, shaking off the bonds of sleep and preparing to start another day. She felt moisture gathering at the corners of her eyes, then sliding down her cheek to the white cotton pillowcase, already stained with circles of tears from last night.

The next morning Marlene awakened, the sun was above the horizon, a bright golden fireball. From somewhere a radio blared out the morning stock report while voices floated up from downstairs.

As Marlene dressed, her heart pounded fast in anticipation of having to face Jesse, but all her qualms dissipated when she glanced out the window and saw him hurrying across the yard in the direction of the stables. She tore her eyes away from his tall, lean body and quickly buttoned the last button on her cool, satiny white blouse, then tied a cheery red scarf at her neck. The belt buckle on the jeans had an inlay of turquoise, mother of pearl, and just enough red coral to pick up the color of the red neckerchief.

She descended the stairs rapidly and managed to smile as she slid onto the bench at the breakfast table beside Mrs. Yancy. In greeting the older woman, she noticed a worried expression on her face.

"Is something wrong?" she asked, snapping her napkin open and reaching for a slice of buttered toast.

Mrs. Yancy sipped her coffee

thoughtfully and slowly shook her head before speaking.

"It's Jesse. He's acting mighty peculiar this morning. Last night too. Seems to have his head in never-never land."

Marlene found the toast suddenly too dry in her throat and had to force it down with a deep drink of orange juice.

"Well," she said after a pause, "maybe he's worried about that mare that was stuck in the mud. She seems to be sick. Did he tell you?"

Mrs. Yancy stared blank-eyed out the window at the panoramic view for several seconds, then inhaled deeply and gazed again at Marlene. She smiled.

"I suppose you're right. He called the vet this morning, first thing. Old Patterson was out on an emergency call in Aledo. His wife didn't know when he'd be back. Guess Jesse was upset because of that." The older woman got up from the table, slapping her hands on her knees. "Well, I reckon the barbecue and all the fun will snap him out of it. The boy needs something to take his mind off work, anyhow." Mrs. Yancy stepped to the nearest window, pressed her face to the cool glass, and studied the sky. "Umn, ummm. Sure hope those

187

thunderheads stay put for a while. We need more rain, that's for sure. But maybe the good Lord will just postpone the flood for a few hours. Then He can let 'er rip." She winked, patted Marlene's back, and then hurried out of the room.

Marlene finished her meal, then strolled to the window, pausing to take in the breathtaking beauty and serenity of the scene below, and also hoping to spot Jesse. But all she saw was the cook and an assistant turning a side of beef over an open pit, and basting the meat with a deep red-brown sauce.

After breakfast, Marlene, Freddy, and Mrs. Yancy rode out together to a small church. Marlene saw several familiar faces, but nothing could take her mind off Jesse, and soon the final hymn was drifting out the opened windows and blending softly with the rustling cottonwood trees outside the old white wooden building. When they returned, she noticed that guests had begun to arrive. Most were young, rather impudent-looking college students, who piled out of Cadillacs and expensive pickups. The boys wore fancy Western clothes from Cutter Bill's, with freshly steamed and creased hats, while the girls wore skin-tight jeans and sequin-studded shirts, whose buttons conspicuously remained unsnapped at the bosom.

Marlene glanced down at her non-Western blouse and felt a wave of discomfort. She prayed the day would hurry and yet dreaded that final moment of departure, for it meant relinquishing Jesse forever.

The people attending the celebration fell into two distinct groups. The younger friends passed the Lone Star beer around and grew more boisterous. The ranch hands, probably invited at the insistence of Mrs. Yancy, kept to themselves, shuffling about, seemingly out of place in their simple work clothes. Marlene kept a constant vigilance for Jesse, but he was nowhere to be seen.

Finally, Mrs. Yancy rang out the call to dinner on a large iron rectangle dangling on the back porch. The guests formed lines to receive the tender smoky flavored beef, hot spicy red beans, and jalapeño-seasoned potato salad. Standing at the end of the line, Marlene suddenly saw Jesse coming out of a nearby barn. She hadn't noticed it before, because of its smallness and run-own condition. She assumed that it was an old building that had been abandoned for one of the larger, cleaner ones. Jesse's sleeves were rolled up to the elbow and his common work shirt was stained with sweat.

Marlene quickly averted her eyes as he glanced in her direction, then looked back up in time to see him give Bonnie Sue a fast birthday kiss on the cheek and in return receive a scolding for being late and dressed so poorly. Heat prickled the back of Marlene's neck at the redhead's nerve, but Jesse's dark searing glare quickly put the young woman in her place, and Bonnie Sue returned to her crowd in a huff.

Marlene watched Jesse closely out of the corner of her eye, always making sure to turn back when he chanced to look her way. He was indeed acting strange – quiet, unfriendly, and aloof. He glanced disapprovingly at the rowdy guests and spoke only to the ranch hands and Mrs. Yancy.

After the meal, the crowd formed teams to try their skills at the various games that had been set up. Not feeling like participating in the festivities, Marlene sat on a large sawed-off tree stump beneath the shade of a pecan tree, sipping quietly on a cola. She had just lifted her gaze upward to study the boiling black clouds moving ever closer when she heard Freddy's familiar voice behind her.

"Well, little lady, you sure ain't having much fun off here by yourself, are you?" He grunted as he squatted down on his haunches and spit a dark stream of tobacco juice onto the sandy soil.

"Hello, Freddy. Well, it's hard to have fun when..." She paused, then smiled. "Oh, no you don't, you old rascal. You aren't going to get me out there acting like an idiot tossing horseshoes." She wagged a finger under his nose and did her best to scowl at him.

Freddy screeched with laughter and he slapped his knees.

"You're too smart fer me, honey pot. Nope. I meant what I said. You look like a little lost doggie out in the rain." His smile drooped and he squinted as he studied her smooth features more closely. "You know, I've been watching another person out here at the doings, and I'd swear he's acting like your identical twin: sitting 'round under trees, avoiding talking to friendly folks, pouting like a spoiled child."

"Freddy..."

"Hush up, gal. Just look at him." The short foreman pointed a calloused tobacco-stained finger toward the tall dark-haired cowboy who was leaning against a tree and watching the horseshoe tossing contest. The lively, laughing crowd urged Jesse to join, but he stubbornly refused.

Freddy shook his head and shifted the tobacco wad to the other side of his jaw. "Now that boy used to be the best tosser round. Why, he's the best at everything he tries. Horseshoes, bronc busting, you just name it. But just look at the derned fool boy. Why, we used to have to hog-tie him down to keep him from getting out there and showing off his talents. Specially to the likes of that orney bunch of yahoos that Bonnie Sue carted out here." He spat fast and hard.

Marlene tried to hid her smile, but soon she was shaking her head and chuckling at the absurdity of Freddy's observations.

"Are you trying to tell me, Fred, that because Jesse's not interested in socializing with the others that his heart's broken?'

"Not just that, sugar lamb. He got skunked at horseshoes while ago, too. Now, I'll admit, he ain't as good as me, but he's sure as shooting better'n those sissy city folks over there. His mind just ain't on his work – er, on his play, that is."

192

Freddy clucked sadly and reached into his shirt pocket, dragged out a hunk of Bull Durham tobacco and sliced off a corner with his knife, carefuly wiping the silver blade on his pants before replacing the rest of the tobacco. He stuffed the dark piece into his right jaw and when he spoke again, Marlene had to strain to make out his words.

"Now, this next contest will be the sure sign of his condition. I realize, being in a crowd of strange folk, the boy might get nervous and lose at tossing the shoes, but this..." He nodded toward a long picnic table where several men had gathered around to sit on the bench. In front of each was a plate covered with piles of green jalapeño peppers. The girls giggled and squealed while the men held their long-neck beer bottles high and cheered their favorite on.

"My gosh, Freddy, are they really going to eat all those hot peppers? Their tongues and throats will be blistered for weeks."

She stood up and walked over. With a sigh of relief, she saw that Jesse was not one of the participants. Dying of a burned-out stomach seemed so much worse than dying of a broken heart.

As the referee shouted "Go," a peal of thunder rumbled the earth, drowning out the yells and screams of the crowd. The seated men began shoving the peppers down, swallowing fast and hard, then taking a drink of beer, being careful not to break the skin of the green fiery ovals, because they knew the hot burning liquid would singe the insides of their mouths and lips and tongue lightning fast.

Freddy had come up beside Marlene and grunted in disgust.

"Hmmp. Ol' Tony Cuellar could down more than all those fellas put together, but he warn't invited. Nobody but Bonnie Sue's college buddies." He spat again.

"Oh ... I didn't know Tony wasn't asked..." The words trailed off as a sudden realization hit Marlene. Maybe Jesse wasn't participating in the events because he was protesting the fact that his ranch-hand friends had been ostracized. A wave of affection and sadness flooded Marlene. She admired Jesse's principles, but regretted finding out he wasn't pining away after her. She felt a blush tint her cheeks and lowered her eyes, turning to go. She returned to the tree stump, and watched the winner of the contest hold high the cheap trophy in the shape of a brass armadillo in one hand and guzzle down cool beer with the other.

Soon the first strains of music started up, followed by cheers from the lighthearted group. It was a fast-moving toe-tapping country song, and soon couples were stomping on the hard, smooth earth.

Marlene smiled to herself as she watched the dancers and listened to the music. The dance styles were different from those of six years ago when she and Jesse had danced underneath the stars in the old courthouse square. And the songs were different too. They were faster, harsher, and the touch of a rock-and-roll beat to them.

Two young men asked Marlene to dance and she politely refused, but she finally gave in and danced a slow dance with Freddy. The little man was in his element when it came to dancing, and as he spun around the floor time and time again with Mrs. Yancy, Marlene thought what a happy couple they made. She noticed that Jesse and Bonnie Sue danced only once, and the young redhead seemed dissatisfied with the results, for she walked off in a rush, leaving him standing alone on the dance floor. Mrs. Yancy came over to speak to Marlene from time to time and finally managed to coax her into joining in as the strains of the Cotton-Eyed Joe screeched in the air. Watching the long line of staggering, laughing men and women weave forward and back, legs kicking in unison, and hips swaying while pressed against each other, Marlene felt a total lonesomeness consume her. She knew that Mrs. Yancy had also coerced Jesse into joining the dance, but he was at the opposite end of the floor, and when the merry tune was over, he broke away and disappeared.

Marlene returned to her secure little spot, breathing heavily after the vigorous dance and drinking down the remainder of her cola. A slow song now filled the air, and in a flash her mind was hurled back to six years ago. She saw herself wrapped tightly in Jesse's warm, strong arms as they danced slowly and rhythmically to the gentle "Tennessee Waltz." It had become "their song" because they had won a little satin ribbon for dancing to it one night and she had proudly worn it pinned to the low scooped ruffles of her peasant blouse. Life was so simple and so beautiful then, she thought. Thinking about those times she couldn't prevent a deep sigh from escaping her.

Marlene looked over the bobbing heads of the dancers, barely visible in the fading evening light, toward where she had last seen Jesse. Suddenly a brilliant flash of lightning lit up the yard and her heart leapt as a pair of dark eyes met hers across the grounds. A shiver shot through Marlene. The silver light had revealed Jesse leaning casually against a tree, his supple body relaxed yet powerful, like a sleeping young lion. Then the light was gone and a deep disturbing crack of thunder drowned out the music.

Someone switched on the overhead light bulbs that had been strung loosely in the swaying trees and that cast dancing shadows over the crowd below.

Soon the wind picked up, bringing with it an unnatural coolness. The red silk scarf at Marlene's neck whipped against her cheeks, and her soft long hair swirled back from her blushing face, but still her eyes could not move from Jesse's shadowy figure. The wind hurled paper cups and napkins across the yard, slinging them against the white picket fence that encircled the ranch house. Chickens huddled under bushes, and the ranch hands had to break up their games and run to secure the stable doors.

Branches on the old pecan trees swished and dipped low as the wind grew stronger, mingling the song of rustling leaves with the sweet country music.

Tiny green pecan hulls dropped in Marlene's lap and she lowered her gaze to brush them away. When she looked up, Jesse was gone. A sharp pain ripped her chest as she desperately scanned the crowd. Couples were retreating to the shelter of the white house, and when a loud crack of thunder and flash of lightning came simultaneously, most of them squealed and dashed inside.

Marlene stood up and folded her arms to ward off the shiver running down her spine and the chill bumps on her skin. Well, she thought, at least I'm free to go back to Dallas. The party's over and nothing can keep me now. She glanced at the musicians one final time. The little brave band continued to play as long as any dancers remained. And a few couples, driven by passion or foolhardiness refused to leave in spite of the now howling wind.

Marlene was tossing her paper cup into a

metal trash barrel, when unexpectedly the strains of the "Tennessee Waltz" floated into the air – soft, mellow, and warm. She froze, her back to the band and the dance floor. She felt something inexplicably powerful moving over her, as if a taut lasso were drawing her against her will. Slowly she turned and, without surprise, saw Jesse standing in front of her. He held out his hand and she gave him hers, and, in silent, mutual consent, they stepped to the dance area.

Mrs. Yancy and Freddy also stepped onto the dance floor. But Marlene saw no one; she heard only the soft melody and baritone singer. The wind whistled through shifting pecan trees, dashing the youngest branches mercilessly and whipping the hair from Marlene's face. But she felt only the strength of Jesse's arms pulling her closer to his warm body. Thunder rumbled again, shaking the earth beneath her feet, but Marlene heard only the thunder of her heart and Jesse's heart as their bodies clung together. Softly, tenderly, she laid her head on his chest and closed her eyes, letting his legs guide her where they wished. The end of the earth could have been only inches away; she didn't care. Nothing mattered but his touch as his gently swaying body communicated a message as old as time and as basic as life to her trembling form.

Soon the first fat cold drops of rain thudded on the hard dirt, dispiriting the remaining dancers. But with Jesse drawing her closer in a protective gesture, Marlene felt the warm isolation of love. Suddenly the rain broke loose with fury, sending the musicians running among curses and laughter. Marlene opened her eyes just as Jesse removed his cowboy hat and crammed it on her uncovered head, then wrapped a muscular arm around her waist and pushed her at breakneck speed toward the small older barn where she had seen him earlier. The rain was sweeping across the yard in a giant silver sheet, churning the ground into a lake of mud, when they dashed inside the weatherbeaten barn.

Marlene removed the hat and gently handed it to Jesse, her eyes all the while studying the face above her and the dark irises that returned her searching look. She started to speak, but his lips quickly caught her words, pressing with a savage tenderness that sent an electrifying bolt through her body. Her pulse leaped forward as she felt the strong, hollow pounding of Jesse's chest against her rain-soaked breasts. A soft moan of pleasure escaped from deep within her throat in response to his lingering kiss and his arms drew her slender form closer until she could feel the pressure of his excitement against her abdomen.

"Oh, Jesse, Jesse..." she stammered between kisses, "I thought you didn't want me. I thought..." Her words died as his lips took hers again, hungrily consuming her mouth while his hands slipped to her wet silky blouse. His hand pulled the damp cloth up until it was freed from her blue jeans, then moved skillfully beneath the loose material to the small of her back. Fiery sensations darted down her spine as his palm massaged her gently, then worked higher and around to the front. Her breasts swelled with throbbing anticipation of the approaching hand. And when the cool fingers found the soft, warm flesh, a little cry of agonizing pleasure rose from her throat.

Without speaking they dropped to their knees onto a pile of soft, yellow straw. Jesse's experienced fingers rapidly unbuttoned the blouse and Marlene's trembling fingers did the same to the wet shirt that clung to his muscular contours. When the blue checked cloth was free, she pushed it aside, letting her fingers rove over the firm tanned chest, slide through the fine dark hairs, and circle the tiny brown nipples.

Jesse lay back, pulling Marlene down beside him. As he blazed a trail of kisses down her cheek, she extended her slender neck to receive the precious warmth that softly moved lower, stopping just at the brown halo of her breast. While his tongue maneuvered over the familiar territory, his hands easily found her belt buckle, then slid away her jeans.

Jesse's slender tanned fingers moved in a tender caress over the sleek curve of her waist, then pushed away the damp blouse, his dark eyes savoring the beauty with a hungry impatience. Marlene felt her heart pounding and a spontaneous flow of soft, tender words left her lips. She leaned closer and kissed his bare chest, then moved her tongue down his hard body to the line of hairs that vanished inside the taut Levis.

Her fingers, quivering with anticipation, unfastened the snap and tugged the zipper free. As if unable to bear the intense pleasure another moment, Jesse let out an uncontrollable moan and rolled over, forcing her slender form beneath his. Marlene felt the weight of his warm perspiring body pressing against her breasts, and his hot breath burning in her ears as he whispered, "I can't fight it anymore, Marlene. I love you. I always have and I always will."

Before her trembling lips could respond, his seeking mouth pressed against hers and his tongue slipped inside.

Soon tender words of love and passion and soft moans of excited pleasure drifted out the barn door to mingle with the pounding rain that whipped against the tin roof. Thunder shook and the lightning lit up the dim straw-covered floor to reveal two silhouettes pressed together in the ancient art of love.

Lulled by the sound of the rain's gentle melody, Marlene snuggled against Jesse's hot body and released a long, satisfied sigh.

"The rain's over," she soon said as she peered at the final falling drops and heard the loud gurgle of water spilling down the gutter into a rusty barrel under the corner eaves. Turning, she saw Jesse's dark eyes studying her face closely.

"I'm sorry I hurt you yesterday," he said. "I was such a fool. I didn't sleep all night. I could hear you crying and my heart was aching. I wanted to bust in the door or climb through your window and take you in my arms and tell you what an idiot I'd been – that I love you even more for having given in to temptation. It only shows that you're a woman in every way. But I was so mule-headed stubborn and full of pride. Marlene..." He took her hand and tenderly kissed the fingertips. "Forgive me, please."

Marlene smiled through glistening eyes.

"It takes a fool to know one, Jesse. Only I have a head start on you because I made the worst mistake of my life when I left you six years ago. I've suffered because of it, but I never realized until now how much you've been hurting over the years too."

Jesse drew her closer, wrapping his arms around her and kissing the top of her hair.

"It doesn't matter now. Nothing matters but the fact that we've finally come to our senses."

They clung to each other in silence for a

long time, then Jesse gently disengaged himself and reached for her blouse. IIe handed it to her almost like a bashful boy.

"We'd better get dressed and get back to the ranch house. Somebody might come looking for us now that the storm's passed."

Marlene nodded and rapidly slipped into the damp clothes, shivering at the touch of the cool cloth against her hot skin. While tying the red scarf around her neck, she scanned the inside of the old building.

"Jesse ... I saw you in here earlier today. What is this place, anyway?"

"This?" he said, following her gaze. "Well, it hasn't been used in years. But when the mare started acting so peculiar, I decided to put her in here, just in case she might have something contagious. Not that it would do much good; she's already been around the other horses too much to prevent anything..." He paused, a worried expression clouding his face.

"The mare's in here now?" Marlene looked around for the familiar brown head with the white blaze. "But where?"

Jesse swirled and pointed, "She's in the last stall and – " He stopped abruptly and stared at the stall. Suddenly he broke into a trot, his boots making deep dents in the sandy soil. When he came to the stall, he grabbed the old cribbed wooden gate.

"Oh, my God!'

Chapter Ten

Marlene dashed to the stall and ground to a halt at the sight of Jesse stooped over the still, damp body of the mare. In a trembling voice she asked, "Is – is she dead?"

"Almost. She's barely breathing; in a coma, it looks like." Jesse gently stroked the damp head, tenderly pushing aside the forelock and lifting the eyelids. "Marlene, tell Jewel to call the vet again. I'll stay here just in case..." He paused and glanced up into Marlene's troubled face. He rose to his feet, took her face in his hands, and kissed her gently on the cheek. "Don't worry. Everything will be all right. She's been inoculated against all the major diseases. It's just probably a gut problem that the vet can fix in a jiffy. Now, go on. Hurry." He squeezed her hands affectionately before pushing her slightly toward the stall's door.

Marlene ran across the dirt yard, unaware of the layer of mud sloshing over the toes of her expensive boots. When she reached the back porch, gasping for air, a group of party guests who had come out after the rain ended stopped chattering and stared at her in bewilderment. She pushed past them on her way to the kitchen, from which the sound of Mrs. Yancy's distinctive laughter came. As soon as she burst in, the laughter ceased and Mrs. Yancy stood up.

"Marlene . . . what's wrong?"

"The mare . . . she's almost dead . . . in a coma. Call the vet." She struggled to catch her breath and was unaware of Bonnie Sue's piercing gaze burning into her back. The red-head's words cut into the silence like falling icicles.

"So that's where you've been. In the barn. And don't try to tell me Jesse wasn't with you."

Marlene swirled around, but Mrs. Yancy caught her by the arm and pulled her aside toward the telephone. "Bonnie Sue, hush up," she shouted and threw her daughter a forbidding glare. Then she pressed her hands into Marlene's shoulders. "Calm down, girl. Old Doc Patterson called a little while ago. He'd just got back from Aledo and read Jesse's message. The old scutter's on his way out here right now. You look all done in. Have a cup of coffee and sit down a spell." Mrs. Yancy put her arms around Marlene's shoulders, led her to the kitchen table, and forced her to sit on the bench. Marlene took the cup of coffee Mrs. Yancy gave her and sipped cautiously, her eyes darting toward the adjoining room, where she could just make out Bonnie Sue's red hair. Mrs. Yancy patted Marlene's free hand.

"Don't fret about Bonnie Sue. She's just in a foul mood because the shindig got rained out. She didn't mean anything by it."

Marlene nodded, but after swallowing the last sip of black liquid, she rose to her feet.

"I've got to get back to Jes – I mean to the mare."

"Now, you're soaked to the bone, girl. Get on upstairs and change into dry clothes or you'll catch pneumonia." She ushered Marlene through the milling crowd and up the stairs, then stood guard over her until she had changed into comfortable dry jeans and a soft red flannel shirt. She tied her damp hair into a ponytail with a red ribbon.

When they had returned downstairs, Marlene noticed that most of the party group had dispersed, leaving deep tire tracks in the muddy drive and yard. Near the older barn, a mud-splattered red van stood.

"Good, good. The vet's here already." Mrs. Yancy pointed to the van and hurriedly accompanied Marlene across the yard.

"Howdy, Jake." The older woman smiled in greeting upon joining Doc Patterson and Jesse in the barn. The veterinarian was a man in his fifties with kind brown eyes that showed a lack of sleep and a tiny stubble of grayish whiskers over his well-formed chin and jaws. He shook Mrs. Yancy's hand and nodded to Marlene.

"Howdy, Jewel. Haven't seen you in ages. Wish it could have been under better circumstances." He lowered his gaze to the mare and Jesse's stooped back.

"Well, Jake, what does it look like?" Mrs. Yancy asked determinedly.

The vet's eyes met the older woman's. He cleared his throat, then ran his large square fingers through his unruly hair.

"Encephalomyelitis," he said in a weary voice.

"Oh, Lordy, no. Are you sure?"

"Nope, course not yet. But the first signs

210

don't look good. I'm sorry, Jewel. I know you've had more'n your share of trouble."

"But how – " The words stuck in Mrs. Yancy's throat, and Marlene felt an icy chill creeping up her spine as she stared at the motionless animal, whose large swollen belly carried a priceless foal. Tears began to glisten in her large green eyes.

"Dr. Patterson," she asked, "what is en ... enceph – whatever it was you said? It sounds so horrible."

"It is. Equine encephalitis. Sleeping sickness. It's spread by infected mosquitoes. The horses get a fever, then go into a deep coma. Most never come out of it."

"But isn't there some kind of medicine ... some kind of inoculation?"

The old man slowly shook his head.

"Wish there was. But once an animal contracts the disease, it can't be cured from a serum. The only way to fight sleeping sickness is preventive medicine. Keeping the horses away from mosquito-infested places, and keeping them vaccinated." He shifted his weight, then knelt down and placed a sun-browned hand on Jesse's broad back. "There's nothing more you can do, son. I've got the spinal tap and blood samples. I'll get them off to the lab as soon as I get home. We won't know for sure if it's encephalomyelitis until the tests are made. In the meantime, try to keep her fever down, and I'll be back first thing in the morning to give her another shot."

Jesse, who didn't seem to have heard the veterinarian's words, ran his fingers through his dark hair and shook his head.

"I don't understand, I just don't. She's been vaccinated against everything, Doc. You know that. The owner is a millionaire. This is his pride. He spared no expense on her. It can't be sleeping sickness. It just can't." Jesse, his eyes dark with worry, faced the veterinarian.

"Jesse, all you have is a slip of paper saying she was vaccinated. Heaven knows what was put into her veins at the crazy mixed-up ranch. He had such a bad turnover – couldn't keep any hired help – no telling what kind of vet was looking out for the mare before she came here."

"Jake, you know what an outbreak of this disease could mean to the quarter-horse ranches around here."

"Yes. I'll never forget the last one. It's ugly."

Jesse leaped to his feet.

"We've got to tell the other ranchers."

"Jesse, wait a minute. We don't know for sure yet. Wait till the results come in. You've got a whole herd here; have any other animals come down sick yet?"

"Not that I know of."

"That's a good sign, so let's just wait. When you find even one more sick horse, let me know and we'll start worrying about the rest of the herds. In the meantime, I'm sorry, but your herd is in quarantine. Those colts you had lined up to sell will have to wait till this is cleared up. Sorry." He gave Jesse a pat on the back and a compassionate nod. "Sit tight, son. And keep an eye on the mare. Let me know if there's any sign of change."

He replaced his battered hat on his head, picked up his black bag, and walked with a slight limp toward the barn door. Marlene stared at Jesse a moment, then darted after the doctor. She caught up with him just as he reached the red van.

"Dr. Patterson? What if the mare does have encephalitis? What then? Will she die?"

"Yep, 'fraid so. One way or another."

"W-what do you mean?"

"Well, if she doesn't die outright from

the disease, she'll have to be shot to death. And any other animals found with the disease, because there's no cure."

"No!" Marlene cried out incredulously.

The vet slid his black bag and the blood samples onto the front seat, then turned to face Marlene before getting into the van.

"But Jesse keeps his herd vaccinated, so I doubt that any other horses will contract it, even if she does have sleeping sickness. Don't fret." He got in the car, then waved as he shifted the rough gears and backed out of the barnyard.

Reentering the barn, Marlene saw a new figure standing beside Jesse, and as her eyes adjusted to the dim light, she realized that it was Freddy. All faces turned to her as she stepped up, and suddenly her heart began to race.

"Is something wrong?" she stammered, her eyes sweeping from worried face to worried face. "Is the mare dead?" She moved closer and looked down. The mare lay still, but the softly rising and falling belly verified that she was still alive. Marlene looked up. "What's wrong, Freddy?"

"I found three more sick horses. One's already on his knees."

"Oh, no . . ." Marlene swung around to face Jesse, only to see him rushing past her toward the door. She felt an empty ache in her chest at the expression of agony on his face. She started to go after him, but Mrs. Yancy pulled her back.

"Let him go. There're times a man has to be alone. Come on. Let's go inside and leave word at the vet's office about what happened. Poor Jake."

Back in her room, Marlene paced the floor like a caged cat, weaving in and out of the packed suitcases and biting her nails. She couldn't leave now, not just when she and Jesse were reconciled, and when he needed her the most. But she had told Vaughn Casstevens that she'd be back in Dallas tonight and back on her job tomorrow morning. Defying him would mean the end of her career. But at the moment she didn't care about that. Her thoughts were of Jesse alone. The passionate lovemaking they had shared in the driving rain now seemed too remote to be real.

Marlene slumped down on the bed and gazed out the window. She was looking toward the stables when she saw Bonnie Sue walking with fast, firm steps toward the house. A smile covered the impish face, and Marlene knew something had transpired between her and Jesse. A strange feeling crept over her, and on a sudden impulse she leaped to her feet and bounded down the stairs to the kitchen. On the back porch she could see Mrs. Yancy in her favorite rocking chair, the dim light of one yellow light bulb casting eerie shadows over the woman's wrinkled and tired face. She was sipping on a cup of coffee, while staring blankly at the stables, which were now mainly a series of bright lights in the fast-approaching dusk.

On entering the kitchen, Marlene heard footsteps in the hallway, as if someone was retreating, but she didn't bother to investigate farther. She lifted the phone receiver and placed a collect call to Vaugn Casstevens.

The voice on the end of the line was sharp. "Yeah?" it demanded, and Marlene's grip on the receiver tightened.

"Hello, hello," the voice snapped again.

"Vaughn? It's Marlene."

"Well. It's about time. Are you home now?"

"Vaughn, something's happened. I – I'm still at the ranch."

"Another accident to a friend?" he asked sarcastically.

"No, I'm serious. One of the horses is almost dead and three more are very sick. The veterinarian thinks it's equine encephalitis – sleeping sickness."

"You don't say." Vaughn's voice began to express interest. "Go on. Is it a deadly disease?'

"Yes. The affected animals will have to be shot. The herd's already in quarantine."

"Terrific!"

"What? Vaughn! I know you don't like Jesse, but that's cruel...."

"I don't mean terrific that his horses are sick. Hell, I don't wish disasters on people. But when I smell one coming, by damn, I'm not going to sit on the sidelines and sob. This has the makings of a great human interest story, don't you see?"

"No, I don't see. This is a tragedy, Vaughn. A man may lose everything he's ever dreamed and worked for. He ran away and joined the rodeo and worked for years breaking his back so he could save enough money to buy a half interest in this ranch. It had just gotten to the point of making a profit. Don't you see what this could mean to him?"

"Marlene, Marlene. Are you forgetting that you're a reporter? Of course, this is a tragedy. That's what makes it news and a great story. Would you have ever heard or cared about the Hindenburg blimp if it'd landed safely?"

"You're callous and ... unemotional and – "

"Marlene, I'm an editor. Don't talk to me about having no emotions. All the fibers of my guts are on fire now screaming to me that this is going to be one hell of a feature. I took this little backwoods magazine and made it into one of the best in the state and country just on gut-felt instincts like this. Now, is there any chance this epidemic might spread to other ranches, to the whole state?"

"It's not an epidemic yet, Vaughn. And it may not be. They aren't sure if it's sleeping sickness. The tests haven't come in – "

"Never mind the details. You can fill me in on it in the morning when you see me there."

"You – you're coming down here? But why?"

"This is a fantastic opportunity. I remember the last outbreak of some kind of swine-type disease. Had to shoot thousands of pigs, dig trenches, and bulldoze them over. Prices shot sky high. It affected the whole country, don't you know. This isn't as sensational, but all Texans love horses. I'll bring Archie along to shoot pictures."

"I have a camera here already."

"And maybe Eileen to take notes – "

"Vaughn! Have you forgotten that I'm a reporter too? I *can* write."

A soft laugh filled the receiver. "You don't seriously think that you could be unbiased on this story, do you?"

"Yes, I do. Probably more unbiased than you."

The answering silence left Marlene uneasy, but Vaughn's voice was warm when he spoke.

"You might be right, angel. I am pretty bisased when it comes to some cowboy trying to horn in on my territory. Actually, I'm pretty anxious to meet him. Size up the competition."

"Vaughn, there's something – "

"Save it, kid. I've got loads of work to do before I hop on down there. I'll see you in the morning. And then we can have a nice long cozy talk. Alone in some remote cow pasture among the hay and cactus. I'll bring your engagement ring for your approval." He chuckled. "*Adios*, angel."

The receiver clicked before Marlene could speak. She held it away from her ear, staring at it as if waiting for an answer. The soft tap that came sent her eyebrows up. She pressed the receiver to her ear again, but heard only silence. Maybe it had been her imagination. She gently replaced the receiver.

Marlene trod the stairs wearily, holding on the worn wooden rail, for there was no light along the staircase. As she reached her room, she saw a pale light coming from under Bonnie Sue's door, which was slightly ajar. She heard the redhead humming merrily, then a low laugh.

She continued on to her room, and was just opening her door, when a voice sang out. "'*Adios*, angel.'" A peal of laughter followed.

Marlene felt the heat rising to her cheeks and she swirled around to face the girl, who had emerged from her room.

"If I were you, Bonnie Sue, I wouldn't be announcing the fact that I listen in on other people's phone conversations."

"Well, you're not me, and I'm sure as hellfire not you, now am I?"

"Thank goodness."

"Well, now." Bonnie Sue leaned back against the hall wall, her arms folded, her impish hazel eyes reflecting the dim overhead hall light. "So you and sweet little Vaughn are just a whole lot more than a boss and his secretary. Now, I kinda figured it was something like that when I found out that was his little sports number straddling the driveway."

"I don't owe you any explanations about Vaughn and me."

"Of course not. I understand how it is. A good-looking man, or maybe not, but at least a filthy rich one. Don't blame you one little bit. And as for Jesse ... why, who on earth could refuse the charms of that gorgeous hunk of a man." Her smile widened as she uncrossed her arms and began to turn.

"Leave Jesse out of this conversation, if you don't mind."

"Oh, I mind all right. Because you see, before you came along me and Jesse had great plans. I'm fixing to graduate from the university next year, and I'll be wanting to settle down with a husband. Now, I've had my eye of Jesse since I was still in braces."

"How well I know."

"And I'm not about to give him up to some old flame that comes back for a weekend visit and gets all lovey-dovey again. You're not going to get him, you hear?"

"I hear. But there's one thing you forgot, Bonnie Sue. Jesse and I loved each other before you even knew what love was. And we still do. That's one thing you'll never be able to destroy."

"No? Maybe not." She moved toward the staircase, her hips swaying in the tight jeans. But once more she stopped and turned. "But I just can't wait to see Jesse's face when he finds out that dear old Vaughn is coming and bringing along your engagement ring. Try explaining that one to him." She tossed her flame-red curls and laughed all the way down the stairs.

Chapter Eleven

Marlene's first reaction was to run after the girl and slap her insolent face. But after a moment's hesitation she realized that she would then be no different than Bonnie Sue, resorting to the tricks of a jealous, immature girl. No, she knew that Jesse's love for her would override any lies and insinuations that Bonnie Sue planted in his mind. The girl was hardly more than a child – surely Jesse would never seriously consider marrying her.

As for Vaughn Casstevens, she would just have to meet him head-on and let him know immediately that the engagement was off. Actually, she had never officially said yes, but he would have to be set straight anyway. It might hurt his feelings, but he would always have his first true love – the magazine.

As Marlene undressed and slipped between the cool cotton sheets, her mind whirled, reliving every second since arriving in Waterford, hearing every angry word from Jesse's lips and remembering every tender touch. Soon her thoughts merged into dreams of Jesse's herd being infected. And worst of all, she saw Vaughn standing over the dead mare, rapidly scribbling the gruesome details while his photographer snapped sinister angles of the lifeless body.

Marlene was suddenly awakened by the sound of loud rapping on her door. She pushed her limp hair back, still damp from the hot, fitful night, and swung her feet to the cold hardwood floor. Before opening the door, she slipped into her satin robe and ran her fingers through the tangled hair.

"Vaughn! What time is it?"

"Ten o'clock in the A.M., sleepy head. I thought farm girls got up with the chickens," he teased, pushing the door all the way open and stepping inside. His intense blue eyes took in the contents of the room in one rapid scan.

"Well, they do. Provided they go to bed with the chickens, too," she replied in a sleep-filled husky voice. She lifted her long hair from underneath the robe collar, and, as she looked up, saw Vaughn's eyes devouring the deep V-neck that teasingly revealed the smooth upper curve of her breasts. She instinctively pulled the cool cloth closer to her, and he raised his gaze to meet hers. Their eyes locked for a brief instant, then he drew in a deep breath, and walked past her, throwing a leather briefcase on the crumpled bed covers.

"We've got a lot of work to do. First, I need all the background material you can find on this horse disease."

"All right. And what about the human interest angle of the story? I think I should handle that too, don't you? I mean, I know all these people, and I understand what they're going through. I *feel* for them."

"Ah, but that's just the point. I don't want you to *feel*. You have to be neutral and unemotional. Investigate and let the facts tell you what to write. You've got to be able to see the story from everybody's side at once."

Marlene had to force herself to keep from blurting out her anger at his lack of confidence in her unbiased reporting.

"I don't recall ever being cited for my slanted journalism. I pride myself on being fair to all sides. And – "

"Sure, sure," he interrupted with a wave of his hand. "When you're interviewing strangers and people you've got no involvement with. But did you ever do a story on your mother or your sister?"

"I don't have a mother or sister," she protested.

"You know what I mean. This case is different. It hits home because you've got a personal slant to it. Maybe it's Jesse's fault that those valuable horses are dying. Maybe he was careless."

"That's not true!"

"But suppose it was. Would you be able to write it up, presenting your old lover in a bad light, knowing he would read it? Would you?"

Marlene, her eyes cast down, experienced a sickening feeling in the pit of her stomach. After a long silence she looked up into Vaughn's clear blue eyes.

"Yes, if it was the honest, indisputable truth."

Vaughn peered into her serious green eyes a long time, then put his hand on her shoulder.

"Okay, kid, the story's yours. You can write it. I'll just serve as adviser and help you with the interviewing."

Marlene let out a deep sigh. "Thanks," she said softly, though she was not sure she meant it.

Vaughn, his back to Marlene, snapped open the latches of the briefcase and shuffled until he had found several sheets of paper, which he placed on the bed. After relatching the leather case, he turned around.

"I trust your talents, Marlene. As a matter of fact, I've been seriously considering you for the associate editorship. You know Clark is leaving pretty soon."

Marlene nodded, her brain numbed by his words. She had dreamed of this possibility the moment she'd heard of Clark's plans to move. Slowly she sank down onto the edge of the bed. Vaughn stepped closer.

"You've got some really tough competition for the position. I know this horse disease story will be a difficult one for you, but your attitude and unprejudiced reporting here could make all the difference and swing the pendulum in your favor."

"Thank you, Vaughn. It'll be a test for me too – in more ways than one."

As she stood up, Vaughn caught her arm, pulled her close, and pressed his lips to hers. She felt his freshly shaven cheek, noticing how smooth and soft it was compared to Jesse's face. She received the kiss, but when she didn't respond, he let her go, a strange expression on his face.

"Now, I think I could have gotten more emotion out of kissing a dead fish," he said lightheartedly, peering at her awkwardly.

Marlene didn't know what to say.

"I'm sorry, Vaughn. I'm still too sleepy and tired to think straight. Besides, if I gave you a real kiss, I'd feel like I was influencing your decision." She hoped her pathetic attempt at deception would be effective, but one glance into Vaughn's eyes told her it had been a miserable failure. But, to her surprise, he merely patted her hand and smiled.

"All right, have it your way. But now you're insinuating that *I* can't be unbiased. Believe me, even if we got married, it wouldn't mean that you'd get the position." He winked. "Shake a leg and get dressed so you can take me down to the stables and show me the layout." He pulled the door to with a firm click, leaving Marlene alone with her confused thoughts.

She stared at the doorknob a moment, a little shocked at his attitude. It had been too easy. He was a considerate man, true, but very stubborn when it came to getting what he wanted. And once again she had passed up the opportunity to tell him she could not marry him. Had his announcement about the promotion affected her? Marlene squeezed her eyelids closed. No. However badly she wanted that position, she would never use Vaughn's affection to obtain it.

With a shiver she rapidly removed the robe and pulled on fresh jeans and an old, worn Western shirt that had belonged to Ginny Yancy. She swiftly applied the barest amount of makeup, then ran a brush through her silky hair.

In the hall Marlene joined Vaughn and Archie, the photographer, a tall man almost as ragged as a scarecrow, with baggy pants that hung on his bony legs and a white shirt that wrinkled at the waist.

First they strolled to the barn that contained the sick mare, Archie rapidly snapping shots of the ranch and surroundings along the way. The mare still lay on the barn floor, her breathing labored and her body wet. Freddy, sitting on an overturned bucket, hovered over her, constantly wringing out water-soaked towels and laying them over her feverish body while a stable boy kept the water buckets filled. Freddy glared at the skinny photographer as he snapped shot after shot of the suffering horse and of Freddy himself. He spat out a defiant stream of tobacco juice, but Archie merely caught the moment on film, to his obvious satisfaction.

"Beautiful!" Archie muttered under his breath. The camera swirled to the next frame, freezing Freddy's set jaw and glaring gray eyes. After a while of Vaughn firing question after the question, the foreman finally stood up with a jerk.

"I ain't answering no more of your foolheaded question. If you want something else, go ask Jesse. Only he ain't in no mood for reporters neither." He snarled the word "reporters" and cast a quick hostile glance at Marlene that made her heart sink.

"Come on, Vaughn, you promised you wouldn't interfere with the work. Freddy's busy, can't you see?" She tugged at his elbow, but the blond man kept scribbling intently on his yellow note pad.

"You too, Archie," she insisted, when the latter kept shooting pictures of Freddy. Finally she grabbed his sleeve and pushed him forcibly away.

"Man, oh, man," Archie said, in his heavy northern accent as they finally walked out of the barn and he expertly changed film. "That old geezer had the most interesting face I've ever seen. Did you see the way he spat that tobacco juice? Must have been fifteen feet at least. Do you think that's some kind of world record?" He continued muttering in this manner while they headed for the newest stable.

On the way, they passed Mrs. Yancy and Bonnie Sue. Both men's eyes homed in on the young woman's swaying hips packed into the skin-tight jeans.

"Amazing!" Archie whistled low under his breath. "It must be the same principle that they use to pack sardines in those little cans."

Vaughn laughed loudly, but Marlene remained silent for they had just reached the stable door. At the far end of the line of stalls, near the large one that belonged to Renegade, she detected Jesse's tall figure. She began walking faster, soon out-stripping the two men, and her ears didn't hear a question Vaughn asked. She saw nothing but the dark eyes ahead communicating silently with her. Her heart pounded loudly as she came closer, and she blushed at the meaning of his glance.

Vaughn and Jesse's eyes held each other for a moment after the introductions, but each man was civil. After several meaningful glances from Marlene, Vaughn took the hint and stepped over to interview the vet while she stayed to interview Jesse. As Archie busied himself taking pictures of the stalls, Jesse slipped his arm around Marlene's waist and pulled her close, his lips tenderly taking possession of hers for a brief moment. She felt her breath come in short, rapid pants and her heart thunder out of control. Her arms yearned to respond, but after a quick glance toward Vaughn, she gently pried Jesse's hands away from her waist.

"Jess, I-I have to work now," she whispered, her eyes searching his. She saw a tiny flicker of fire on their black depths, but he smiled and released her, then knelt over Renegade.

"Sure. Go ahead and do your job."

The iciness in his voice froze the words that had started to come to her tongue and for several seconds she stood in silence. Then, like a soldier facing the inevitable battle, she flipped on the small portable tape recorder she was carrying and began asking questions. Some of the questions were painful, both to her and Jesse, but she forced them out, trying to keep her voice as sympathetic and calm as possible. The calmness in her tone, however, only served to irritate Jesse more, and by the middle of the interview she could see that he would not be able to hold his temper much longer.

"Just one more question, Jesse," she said softly, even though she had many more. "Is it possible that all this could have been prevented if the mare's inoculation papers had been checked more closely?"

The silence grew, and only the whirling sound of the black machine filled the air. Marlene felt her face turning hot and at the same instant saw Jesse's right hand clench. His dark eyes went black. Slowly he stood up to his full height and glared down at her.

"I think you've asked enough questions for one day, Miss Whitney." He swirled around, and with a courage bordering on foolhardiness, she called out to his tense back.

"I'm just doing my job, Jesse. Don't take it personally." She trotted up to him, waiting for him to turn. When he did, the dark eyes met hers and a spark of black electricity shot through the early morning air. "Please, Jesse, I *had* to ask those questions. Don't you understand?" She tried to put her hand on his arm, but he jerked it away.

"I understand all right. It's beginning to look to me like your job is the number-one love in your life."

"No . . ."

"If you'll excuse me, I've got twenty sick horses and a hell of a lot of more important things to do than talk to you."

Jerking his hat down on his brow and throwing one final angry dart her way, he moved off and stormed out of the stables.

"Oh, you're so bullheaded," she muttered, watching him disappear. Turning back, she bumped into Archie, almost knocking him over. He smiled, but the expression in his watery eyes was morose. "What's wrong?" she asked softly.

"Oh, nothing, I guess," he said in a low voice, pushing up the gold-rimmed glasses that habitually slid down his long straight nose. "It's just that it depresses me to be around all these sick horses. Look how beautiful they are. Every one looks like something out of a movie. Like Black Beauty or something. And that one mare's pregnant." He heaved a deep sigh, and his bony fingers, as delicate as a butterfly's antennae, toyed with the camera slung around his neck. As his soft, sad words sank in, Marlene peered again in the direction in which Jesse had disappeared. Suddenly her heart wrenched at the thought that she had been less sympathetic to Jesse's problems than a total stranger. If a person like Archie, who had never been closer to a horse than watching a John Wayne movie, could feel such sorrow, what depths of pain would Jesse be in, who loved and worked beside the animals every day?

Shoving the tape recorder into Archie's hands, she raced away to find Jesse and apologize. But he was nowhere to be found. None of the ranch hands or Mrs. Yancy could tell her where he was or even where he had last been seen. Moreover, the fact that Bonnie Sue was also unaccounted for left Marlene more anxious than ever. It was with great effort that she forced herself to drive out to the veterinarian's office and rummage through his library, reading up on equine encephalitis. Every picture of a dead horse left her with a hollow ache in her chest, but she made herself continue until she had all the gruesome details.

Then she visited neighboring farmers, interviewing them about their present fears and their past experience. By the time she returned to the Yancy Ranch it was dark and she almost felt too weary to eat the supper spread out on the table. Only the sight of Jesse's back and dark hair made her decide to stay.

As she deposited her briefcase and note pads on a nearby table Marlene realized that the chattering group had grown quiet. All eyes swung to her, and the smug look on Bonnie Sue's face, along with the questioning, hurt expression on Jesse's, told her the worst.

She greeted everyone and slipped into her place on the bench next to Vaughn, giving him a searching look which he chose to ignore.

The chatter slowly resumed, with Mrs. Yancy beginning to speak of a topic obviously far removed from the earlier one. Without warning, Jesse leaped to his feet and, after giving Marlene a deep, penetrating glare, grabbed his hat and stalked away. Marlene felt her heart roll over and started to rise, but a heavy hand pressed her knee, forcing her down. Eyes shifted nervously from face to face, and finally Bonnie Sue cleared her throat and ended Marlene's doubts.

"Well, Marlene, I don't know why everyone is being so tight-lipped. But I don't mind being the first to congratulate you."

"Congratulate me?" Marlene repeated weakly, turning to Mrs. Yancy for moral support.

"Why, don't be so modest," Bonnie Sue continued. "Any woman alive would be proud to land a catch like Mr. Casstevens here." She lowered her long eyelashes and gave Vaughn her most tantalizing look, her pouty lips curled into a sinister smile. "And that ring. Why, it's big enough to choke a mule, and about the most gorgeous thing I ever laid eyes on. Makes Elizabeth Taylor's old diamond look pitiful." She drawled the words out, watching Marlene's face go pale.

"What ring?" Marlene whispered dryly, turning to Vaughn.

"Oh, no!" Bonnie Sue faked an apology. "I got so excited over that pretty thing, I plumb forgot it was supposed to be a surprise. I hope you'll forgive me, Vaughn ... uh, I mean Mr. Casstevens." She smiled at him enticingly.

"Vaughn!" Marlene leaped to her feet so quickly that she knocked her knees against the underside of the table. "How could you! There's no engagement and you know it. Tell them!" She pointed at the group gathered around the table in stunned silence.

Vaughn, his own pale cheeks turning pink, glanced around at the expectant faces, then sighed. "She's right, folks. It never was official; just a lot of wishful thinking on my part. Marlene . . ."

Marlene spun on her heels and ran from the room before he had time to apologize or before she could see the expression of defeat on Bonnie Sue's face.

Her legs took her as fast as they could down the back porch steps and across the yard and down the hill to the distant small barn where the mare was quartered.

Her lungs ached for air, but she refused to stop until she had stumbled to a halt near the mare's stall, where Jesse stood with his legs spread in a defiant stance.

"Jesse!" she cried between gasps. "Oh, Jesse, please, please listen to me." She tried to latch on to his shirt sleeve, but before her fingers could make contact, he grabbed her arms and shook her.

"You lied to me. After all the love and tenderness. It's the cheapest shot in the world – using a man."

"No, Jesse, you're wrong. So wrong. Listen to me, please."

"What, and hear another pack of lies? No thanks! You can turn around and get out of here. And get out of my life!" With gritted teeth, he gave her a little shove which was enough to make her fall to the sandy floor.

"Wait! Vaughn was the one lying!" she shouted. The words sounded empty as they drifted into the night air and out the barn door after Jesse's tall, rapidly fading silhouette.

Wiping the tears from her eyes, Marlene staggered to her feet and dragged her aching body to the door, from when she watched Jesse stride to the old bunkhouse where he had slept as a young ranch hand. She could make out someone's face, probably Freddy's, in the window, then heard the door open and slam with a bang.

Mustering all the energy she possessed, Marlene trotted over to the white cottage covered with a luxurious rambling queens's wreath vine. She stared at the finely formed heart-shaped leaves and thought of her own heart, so full of agony. Then, with a deep intake of air, she knocked on the screened door until her knuckles stung. As she had expected, Freddy's face popped out the door.

"Howdy, little lady."

"Hello, Freddy. Is Jesse in there?"

"Well, now." He puckered his lips, then winked. "I guess I didn't reckon you came up here to visit the likes of me. Yep, he's here. But I'm warning you, he's more ornery than a wounded coyote right now. Might just decide he wants your pretty little head for his supper." He placed a weathered hand on Marlene's arm and gently tugged her inside while lightly kicking at an overly friendly hound dog that tried to nose its way inside the open door.

Marlene looked around the little comfortable cottage. The living room consisted of old sofas, slightly smelly with grease and age, and one rocking chair. On the wall hung oval-framed photos, long since faded. Over one worn but comfortable sofa a bright crocheted afghan had been slung, and Marlene recognized Mrs. Yancy's handywork. Empty coffee cans sat at various spots, each stained dark and reeking with the smell of discarded tobacco juice and wads. A little portable TV perched on top of a bookshelf dominated the far end of the room, and on the couch, his long legs propped up on a wooden coffee table, sat Jesse.

Marlene timidly inched forward until she stood over him, waiting for him to look up. She could hear Freddy's endless chatter behind her, but the words barely sank in.

"Yep, like I was just telling Jess. Can't imagine why that little fella run off. Ha!" Freddy snorted and laughed at the same time. He was holding a wet plate in his hand and drying it off with a towel. "Always made me feel good being round the boy. We all called him Shorty. Imagine anybody being as short as me. Didn't work more'n a month at the most..." Freddy suddenly stopped talking as he watched Marlene standing over Jesse, waiting. He cleared his throat and then vanished into the kitchen.

Marlene looked at Jesse's profile, her heart aching, waiting for him to respond. It was futile. So she knelt and placed a hand softly on his shoulder. Like a horse flicking away an annoying fly, he jerked his shoulder free and removed his legs from the table.

"Jesse, please don't be so stubborn. I don't know exactly what was said at the supper table tonight, but don't you think I ought to at least be allowed to defend myself since I wasn't there? You're a fair man with a sense of justice. Tell me what Vaughn said and let me either deny or agree. Please." She laid her hand gently on his thigh and silently prayed. After a long pause, his black eyes met hers.

"Okay. He said you were engaged. Then he produced a diamond the size of a fist to back it up."

"I've never seen that ring, I swear."

"I know. He said it was going to be a surprise for you. Hoped you liked it, but that if you didn't, he could trade it in for a bigger one. Hell..." Jesse shifted his weight and stretched a hand toward the front door. "This whole ranch isn't worth as much as that piece of rock. You'd be a fool to turn him down."

"Jesse!" she gasped. "You let me decide what kind of fool I want to be. I'm not engaged to Vaughn. I'll admit that he did propose and he even told me over the phone that he was looking at rings. But I *never* said I'd marry him and now he knows

I never will."

"No? Well, he seems pretty confident."

"Oh, that's just Vaughn. He's confident about everything he ever tries."

"And I guess he's used to winning a lot or else he'd have that confidence knocked down a notch or two by now."

"Well ... yes. Vaughn has a knack of getting what he wants. But not this time."

"Not this time, huh?" Jesse repeated with a slight sarcasm to his voice. "Say, Freddy," he called out, "is this the latest issue of *Texas People Magazine* here on your coffee table?"

In a few seconds the older man ambled to the kitchen door, an apron tied around his spindly waist and his sleeves rolled up to the elbow to reveal white flesh that contrasted with his dark tanned hands.

"Yep, I reckon it is. That's Jewel's magazine. I forgot to give her the mail today after I fetched it because of everything being so agitated. Guess I'll carry it on up there right now if you two want to be alone." He began untying the apron strings and walked across the room, his boots thudding on the thin, worn circular rug.

"You didn't happen to catch the story on

page eleven, did you?" Jesse asked. He picked up the magazine and flipped it open.

"Why, no. I ain't had a chance to look it over yet. Is it one of Marlene's stories?"

"Ummm, you might say that. It's Marlene's story, all right. Here, I guess you might want to read it too," Jesse said. He shoved the magazine into Marlene's arms and stood up. As her eyes scanned the column, she heard Jesse's retreating footsteps. Suddenly a photo leaped up at her eyes.

"Oh, no!" she whimpered. She saw her own face, smiling broadly, next to a picture of Vaughn who was also smiling. Beneath the photos was a caption:

"Good news department. Our own editor-owner, Vaughn Casstevens, proudly announces his engagement to Marlene Whitney, one of our staff reporters. No date has been set yet, but if their faces are any indication, it won't be long. Congratulations to both of you."

The magazine slid from Marlene's fingers. She heard Freddy stoop over and lift the periodical, then the sound of his moving lips as he laboriously read out loud in the dim lamplight. Then slowly he put

244

the magazine back on the coffee table. After a long moment of silence, he returned to the kitchen.

Though she fought with all her willpower, Marlene could not prevent a deep sob from rising to her throat. A shudder ran through her slender frame as she heard the sound of Jesse's pickup motor starting, then the spew of gravel as the wheels sped away.

Chapter Twelve

For a moment Marlene remained still. Then a sudden surge of frustration and anger rushed over her like a tidal wave. Leaping to her feet, she charged out the door, magazine in hand, rushing by the hound dog, which wagged its tail eagerly, and across the yard to the ranch house. She burst through the back door and bounded up the stairs, taking two of them at a time, until she reached Vaughn's room. Her closed fists impatiently banged on the hardwood door. Finally she heard a chair scrape across a bare floor and footsteps approach. The door opened a crack to reveal one bright blue eye.

"Marlene. Come in, come in. I want to apologize for what happened. You know Bonnie Sue was wrong in assuming I said we were engaged. She just jumped to conclusions. What I really said..." His words trailed off when he saw the expression on Marlene's unflinching face.

"Never mind about the ring, Mr.

Casstevens. I want you to explain this."
She shoved the magazine in his face, its
front page folded back so that the column
with the photograph stood out.

Vaughn leaned back, then took the
periodical and held it out far enough away
from him to read. Slowly he lowered it and
his pale face turned even whiter.

"Oh, no! I completely forgot about this.
I had this added 'rush' to the layout weeks
ago. At the time I was sure you'd say yes."
With a crestfallen expression, he moved
back into the room and slumped to the bed,
then glanced up at Marlene. "No wonder
you're so mad. I hope Jesse didn't see
this."

"As a matter of fact he did. Oh, Vaughn,
what a mess you've gotten me into," she
said, no longer angry, dropping down on
the bed beside him.

Vaughn let his hands fall between his
knees and heaved a long, heavy sigh. Then
his eyes suddenly lit up and he dashed to
the briefcase, unlocking it and retrieving an
expensive box. He snapped the lid open to
reveal a patch of black velvet. He held the
box timidly in front of Marlene's face like a
bad little boy's peace offering.

"How do you like the ring? It's yours if

you want it. I know you like rubies and diamonds." He pushed the box closer to her, allowing the overhead light to shimmer off the brilliant diamond surrounded by an exotic pattern of tiny rubies.

"I don't want it. Take it back."

"I can't. It was custom made for you."

"Then I'm sorry. I guess you'll just have to find another finger of the same size that likes rubies and diamonds."

Vaughn stared at the box a long time, then closed it with a gentle click. He then once more slowly retreated to the bed.

"All right, I know when I'm licked. I guess I never really thought you'd give him up for me. Hell, what's a million bucks or two compared to – to all this." He waved his hand toward the opened balcony door.

Marlene felt a sudden uncontrollable laugh building up, and before she could stop it, it rang out loudly.

"What's so funny?"

"Oh, nothing. Just that a few minutes ago another man did the same thing. Waved his hand over the ranch and said 'What's a mere ranch compared to a million bucks?' Men!"

Vaughn glanced at her, his chin resting in his hand. Then, after a heavy, lengthy silence, he stood up.

"Don't worry, Marlene. I'm going to get things straightened out between you and Jesse. It's the least I can do. I'll go to him and explain that the magazine article was a misprint, that I jumped the gun, and so on. It'll be the finest apology that ever passed human lips and tickled human ears." He placed his hand under Marlene's chin, raising it slightly, and kissed her tear-stained cheek.

Marlene smiled through blurry eyes.

"Thanks, Vaughn. Go tell him now. He's probably at the only bar in town." She stood up, urging him to go, but Vaughn refused to budge.

"Not now. I've got work to finish. Besides, getting into a barroom brawl with a bunch of drunk cowboys is the last thing I want. I'll tell him first thing in the morning. Give him time to simmer down."

"But – "

"Now listen. You don't expect me to carry this nice-guy thing too far, do you? I'm starting to get nauseous as it is just thinking about how wonderful and sporting I'm being about the whole mess."

He squeezed her hand, then turned her around and pushed her gently out the door.

"Don't worry, I'll talk to him as soon as the roosters crow. Promise." He held up his fingers, imitating the boy scout signal, then shut the door.

Marlene tossed and turned all night, keeping track of the time by the loud clicking clock on the bureau. About 3:00 A.M. Jesse's pickup drove up to Freddy's cottage, and soon afterward she heard the soft melodic strains of a guitar floating up from the stables. It brought back a flood of sad memories, for she knew that Jesse only played the melancholy tunes when he was in a pensive mood. She struggled not to go to him. Dare she take a chance that he would listen to reason even before Vaughn had explained the magazine article? She got dressed, but as she stood on the balcony, the cool night breeze whipping her hair, her heart cowered in her chest. Finally, as the clock chimed 4:00 A.M., fatigue won over and she returned to bed. She closed her eyes and let the sound of crickets, the gentle, muffled clicking of Vaughn's portable typewriter, and the low notes from Jesse's guitar lull her weary brain to sleep.

She awakened with a start and out of habit turned to the clock.

"Oh, no!" she exclaimed, staring in disbelief at the hands, which pointed to ten o'clock. She leaped to her feet and dressed quickly before scurrying to Vaughn's door. She knocked loudly, then when he didn't respond, entered and scanned the room. Still tying a silk scarf at her neck, she bounded down the stairs to the kitchen, only to find it deserted except for the cook.

"Guadalupe, where is everybody?"

"*Buenos dias*, Señorita Marlene." The woman nodded, her large black eyes giving Marlene's appearance an approving twinkle. "Everybody's down the stables, working to save horses. *Madre mia*, how I pray the big one, Renegade, does not die. Jesse worked so long and so hard to make this ranch a good one. And if these horses don't get well soon . . . ah, *madre mia*." She crossed herself and shook her head sadly. "Here, you sit and let me fix you some breakfast. You look so tired and hungry." She gave Marlene's elbow a shake and pushed her toward the table. But Marlene stumbled out excuses and moved away. As she passed the breakfast table, she spied the familiar magazine with its cover folded back to reveal the mocking photograph. A sense of panic and urgency crept through

251

her heart and she pushed the screen door open and broke into a trot.

She searched the terrain for the sight of Vaughn. Where could he be? Had he talked to Jesse yet? A myriad of unanswered questions swirled through her head as she entered the small barn first, which was deserted except for one stable hand watching the mare and soaking her with wet blankets. Quickly, Marlene walked on to the newest stables.

She stood in the entrance, waiting for her eyes to adjust to the subdued light. Then she heard the unmistakable sound of Bonnie Sue's voice coming from the direction of Renegade's stall, followed by Jesse's voice. As she walked closer to the stall, her heart thudded louder and she found her lips moving in a silent prayer that the champion stud was still alive. His death would mean the sure ruin of the ranch and everything Jesse had dreamed of.

She blinked until her eyes brought the shadowy figures into focus. Then her heart stopped at the unexpected sight of Bonnie Sue and Jesse bent over Renegade, their shoulders touching and their heads close together. She walked nearer. A sudden series of brilliant flashes and the familiar buzz of Archie's camera diverted her attention for an instant. Then she saw Vaughn's blond hair over the top of a horse stall where he was stooped over for some reason.

As Vaughn rose, he spotted Marlene and hurried to her side, carrying a portable tape recorder in his hands. He stopped in front of her and held out the machine, a pathetic expression on his face.

"Dern this thing," he muttered, his large fingers fumbling with the jammed cartridge. "Here, you try it. Your fingers are skinnier than mine." He planted the take recorder in her hands. Marlene placed a hand on the black box unattentively and whispered, "Did you tell him?"

"What?"

"Did you tell Jesse about us? You know, that we're not engaged. That the article in the magazine was wrong."

"Oh, yeah. Sure I told him – about thirty minutes ago." He never took his eyes of the malfunctioning machine. "Hurry up, I need to get this interview going. I overslept like a fool this morning. You too, I guess." He glanced up, then paused. "What's wrong? You look sick."

"Y-you told Jesse already?"

253

"Sure, I promised you I would, didn't I?"

Marlene gazed across the stable toward Jesse, sweeeping his tall, lean physique and coming to rest on his troubled dark eyes. At that moment he turned around and the look he gave her was undeniably one of hostility and aloofness.

"H-how did he react?" she asked, forcing her eyes back to Vaughn in time to see him shrug.

"He didn't, really. Just said, 'Hmm, I see,' then walked off."

"But his eyes, Vaughn, what did his eyes say?"

"His eyes?" Vaughn raised an eyebrow and shrugged again. "Guess I wasn't paying attention. Say, are you going to fix that contraption or not?"

Marlene looked at the tape recorder, heaved a sigh, and quickly used her nails to unsnap the stuck cartridge. She handed it back to Vaughn, who quickly sped away to the end of the stable, where she could see men busily working over the sick horses. The animals were no better and now all the horses quartered in the new stable were ill, though the ones in the older stable across the way were still healthy. Every available hand worked around the clock helping, but the regular duties of the ranch couldn't be shirked. The heavy rain had washed away a section of ground, loosening a fence and allowing a bunch of curious cattle to wander off. The men had to round them up and would be gone during the day.

Marlene stood in a corner of the stable watching people hurry by, as well as Freddy and Mrs. Yancy at one end and Bonnie Sue and Jesse at the other. Bonnie Sue was still kneeling beside Jesse, her sleeves rolled up, her freckled face tense while they worked over the horse, giving him an injection. Soft words passed between the couple, and every command Jesse gave, the girl obeyed rapidly, efficiently, and without question. Marlene caught the look of gratitude in Jesse's eyes when they stood up and saw him put his arm on the young girl's shoulders and say thanks. He didn't even seem to notice Marlene standing in the corner as they rapidly moved on to the next horse.

With a twinge of jealousy, Marlene recalled Jesse's words under the oak tree by the river: " . . . you couldn't ride a horse worth a hoot; you didn't know one kind of cow from another . . ." She glanced down at her city clothes and slender soft hands unused to anything more active than hitting typewriter keys. And her physique, though healthy, was far from what could be considered strong. Bonnie Sue, on the other hand, easily rode horses for hours at a time while doing strenuous maneuvers around barrels and poles. She'd been a tomboy since childhood, and Marlene had seen her chase down and hogtie a calf as well as any boy could. Wasn't Bonnie Sue everything a rancher needed in the way of pioneer-stock womanhood? She seemed the type that thrived on hard times, coming to life in a crisis just like this one.

Marlene's thoughts were abruptly interrupted by the sound of Jesse's voice. She looked up to see him standing beside a horse that wobbled on unsteady legs.

"What did you say?" she asked.

"I said would you toss me that hackamore," he called out again while trying to keep the horse calm.

"H-hackamore?" Marlene glanced around her as she pivoted, her eyes scanning the line of various equestrian tackle slung over a rail and hung on the wall. She stepped closer to the equipment, determined to decipher what it was he wanted. But a wave of futility swept over her and she turned back. "I-I'm sorry, but I don't know what it looks like."

"Never mind," Jesse said as he saw Bonnie Sue coming out of a nearby stall. He let a sharp whistle, then shouted, "Red, go get me a hackamore. Hurry."

Bonnie Sue quickly dropped what she was doing and pranced in front of Marlene, reaching around her to grab a halter with a big, soft nosepiece.

"Excuse me, honey," she said smugly and leaned closer until the fragrance of heady perfume filled Marlene's nostrils.

Marlene's face turned red and, as she moved out of the way, a stable boy bumped into her, dropping his load.

"I'm sorry," she stammered. She got down on her knees to help him gather the spilled items. When she looked up, Jesse was towering above her, arms crossed. "I'm sorry, Jesse, I didn't see him. I just came down here to help. What can I do? Fetch buckets of water or wipe down the horses or . . ."

"It isn't necessary for you to be down here." His voice dropped through the air like icicles.

"But you need every able body you can

get. I can help," she pleaded, her green eyes searching his rock-hard face for some sign of softness. The touch of a hand on her shoulder made her jump. She turned to see Mrs. Yancy.

"Come on, girl. I can put you to use over here," the older woman said, her blue eyes stern and accusing as they met Jesse's. For a moment they continued to stare at one another, then without a word, Jesse returned to the other end of the barn and led the horse away.

An aching feeling consumed Marlene's chest. But as she threw herself into the task that Mrs. Yancy had assigned, soon the ache of her body muscles overrode any feelings of self-pity. By noon her legs trembled with fatigue and her hands were covered with blisters from carrying bucket after bucket of water. Out of the corner of her eyes she saw Bonnie Sue and Jesse working together like an experienced team. Neither of them seemed to be tired or at all worn out.

Soon Guadalupe hustled into the stable, carrying a large basket filled with sandwiches. Marlene stood up and stretched her weary bones, pushing back her hair, which by now was coated with dirt and grease. Her silk blouse had a rip in the sleeve and the designer jeans were smeared with black grease that would never come out. Taking a sandwich, she tried to unwrap the cellophane when pain shot through her hands. She saw her fingers trembling with hunger and knew that she would not be able to work much longer. Laying her hands palm side up on her lap, she stared at the throbbing pads. A shadow then crossed her knees. She gazed up to see Jesse's eyes black with anger.

"What the hell are you trying to do?" he demanded as he dropped down to his knees and seized her hands. He gripped her wrists painfully, then left her for a moment but soon returned with a tube of salve. He gently smoothed the ointment over her blisters, then he carefully wrapped her hands in white gauze which he pinned securely. He slung her hands back to her sides and stood up.

"Now I want you to get out of here."

"But I can still help," she protested, rising to her feet wearily.

"Look, Jewel's too nice to tell you, but, damn it, you're just in the way. When are you going to learn that you're not needed here? Go back to your room and push a pencil around for a while. That's what you're best at, isn't it?" The anger in his voice left Marlene speechless. A sharp lump rose to her throat and her green eyes misted over. Finally, with all the courage she could muster, she insisted, "But, Jesse, I want to help."

"Then just get out. Go back to Dallas and your city life."

"But the story..." she stuttered in confusion and pain.

"Damn the story! Can't you see the horses are dying? Who the hell wants to read about a pile of dead horses. Go back to Dallas, to the pleasant life of airconditioning where nobody sweats or stinks and nobody's clothes get dirty." He turned away, bumping into Vaughn and Archie, who had stepped closer to listen to his outburst.

"But surely you aren't kicking us off the ranch?" Vaughn asked, trying to be as sincere and pleasant as possible. But Jesse's black eyes stopped his smile cold.

"Yes I am. Get off my ranch, all of you." After a last agonizing look at Marlene, he stalked out of the barn.

Chapter Thirteen

Marlene, Vaughn, and Archie tramped up the staircase in deep gloom. Inside Marlene's room, they heaved simultaneous sighs.

"Well, that's that," Vaughn said with finality, tossing the tape recorder onto the bed and lying down himself. The other two sat down on the edge of the bed. "You blew it, Marlene."

"Me?"

"Sure. If you'd just stuck to helping me with the story, taking notes, interviews, research, and so on instead of trying to fit in where you don't belong, none of this would have happened."

Marlene opened her mouth to protest, then slowly hung her head, staring blankly at her bandaged hands. Perhaps Vaughn was right, she thought.

A knock sounded at the door and all three heads looked up. Archie quickly opened the door and faced an apologetic Mrs. Yancy. She walked in unhesitatingly.

"Jewel . . ." Marlene rose to her feet.

"Sit, sit. I know you're worn to a frazzle, girl. I just come to say you can ignore what Mr. Jesse Franklin said down here a while ago. Just a typical Franklin temper tantrum. I own half this ranch and, doggone it, nobody's gonna order *my* guests off without my say-so. You all go ahead and finish your story; you've already put so much work in to it, it wouldn't be right to send you packing now." She smiled through tired, weary eyes.

Marlene walked over to her and flung her arms around her.

"Thanks, Jewel. You're an angel."

Mrs. Yancy grinned her toothy smile. "I'll bring you up some sandwiches."

As the older woman started to gently close the door behind her, Marlene told her to wait a moment and joined her in the hall.

Mrs. Yancy's sincere blue eyes studied Marlene's face carefully.

"I think I know what you want to talk about, hon. Let's go get the food together and talk on the way."

"I'm so worried. I mean about the ranch and the horses. When will the tests be coming in?" Marlene asked as they descended the stairs.

"First thing in the morning, we hope."

"What if it is sleeping sickness?"

"Then it's the end of everything. No horse ranch can survive an epidemic like that. It'd take too many years to get back on our feet. I reckon me and Jesse'd be lucky if we found somebody to buy the property at half price, too. That wouldn't pay off a smidgen of bills after losing the herd."

"But this is your home, Jewel. You lived here forty years. You can't sell."

The older woman shook her head and tried to smile, but her quivering lips refused to cooperate.

"Oh, I'll survive. I always have. Times were worse than this during the Depression. My pa lost every cent he owned and all we had was the stitches on our back – flour-sack dresses, at that. But we came out of it alive, and even managed to have one or two fond memories. Hard times build character, I always say."

Marlene absentmindedly placed sandwiches and potato chips on paper plates while Mrs. Yancy filled tall glasses with iced tea.

"Well, I agree with you. But why can't Jesse see that too?"

"Girl, let me tell you something. That boy has a heart of gold but a stubborn streak of pride a mile long. I guess I'm not telling you anything new. But he's so afraid that he's losing you, he can't think straight."

"But the way he's been treating me lately, I can't help but think he never really wanted me in the first place."

"Ah, shoot, you don't mean that. There ain't two souls on the face of the earth more meant for each other than you and Jesse."

"But he's been acting – "

"Like a born fool. I know it. But didn't you ever touch a snail on its antenna? Didn't the little rascal draw up inside its shell for fear of getting hurt? That's all he's doing. He's so sure that you want the city life more than his kind of life that he won't even give you the chance to say no. You know how men are when it comes to getting rejected." She winked and patted Marlene's back. "Now go on up there and get that story finished. I know it'll be a good one. And have faith in the good Lord. I know everything's gonna be all right. Somehow." She smiled bravely and winked again, pushing Marlene toward the stairs.

As Marlene entered the bedroom, the

eerie silence was the first thing she noticed. Then she saw Vaughn propped up against the bedstead, his dark-framed reading glases on his lap.

"Here's the food," she said.

"Shhh." Archie put his finger to his lips. "He's reading your manuscript."

"But it's still just a rough draft. We haven't gotten all the story in yet, you know."

At that moment, Vaughn laid the last page down and slowly removed his glasses. He quickly ran his index finger under each eye and sniffed before leveling his gaze at Marlene. She held her breath, waiting for him to speak.

"Great, Marlene, absolutely magnificent. I can't remember ever being more touched by a story in my life. Even if the horses pull through, what a beauty of a story. The way you painted a picture of Jesse as a young man, a dirt-poor orphan fighting and kicking his way to the top. It's perfect." He scooped the papers up and stood up. "Marlene, I'm proud of you, and ... well, what can I say? The associate editor position is yours."

Her mouth fell open in shock and her eyes widened as the impact of his words

265

sank in. Suddenly she let out a little squeal and threw her arms around his neck. "Thank you," she said. Then she stepped back, her face and cheeks hot with emotion.

"Does that mean you'll take it?" Vaughn asked, his voice rising slightly.

Marlene slowly sank into the chair nearest the bed. "I-I don't know. I mean, I want it, but – "

"But love is more important, right?" Archie said as he stepped over and tenderly kissed her forehead. "Congratulations, kid, even if you don't take it."

"I-I think I ought to talk it over with Jesse first. I mean, after all..." She paused, not sure what she meant.

"Even after the way he treated you a while ago?" Vaughn asked in irritation.

"Yes, even after that, Vaughn. If there's one thing I've learned from my past stupid mistakes, it's to give every person a second chance, no matter how much they may have hurt you. Every man and woman has his own reasons for doing what he does, and, who knows, he may regret it just as much as you do."

Vaughn glanced at Archie then shrugged.

"I think I'm going for a nice, long drive in the country. Care to come along, Arch? Maybe we can find some social life down at the local saloon."

"Sure thing, boss. Looks like Marlene has a lot of heavy, hard thinking to do."

The men stared at her, but she didn't notice as she closed her eyes and slowly began rocking to and fro in the chair. Soon the swirling thoughts faded into oblivion and the sweet refuge of sleep overpowered her weary body and mind.

When Marlene opened her eyes, again she saw darkness and heard the clock chimes ringing out eleven o'clock. Beads of perspiration clung to her face and body. She rose with a little groan and stepped out onto the balcony. The fragrant air softly swirled around her flushed face and lifted her damp hair from her sticky neck like a mother's cool, soothing hand. The house was dark, but the barn's distant lights shone – a reminder of the vigil going on inside. When the night breeze suddenly shifted directions and a whippoorwill sang out its sweet, sad song, in a flash Marlene was nineteen again, lying on the banks of the Brazos River, snuggled warmly in Jesse's strong arms, listening to the sad refrains of the night birds and counting the silver stars overhead. Suddenly she could no longer hold back the surge of emotion that swept over her. No other man on earth had ever made her feel like that, and she knew no other man ever would.

She turned away from the balcony and rushed down the stairs and out the back door toward the small barn where the mare slept. She drew a mental picture of Jesse keeping vigil over the sick horse like a father over a child, and her heart raced like thunder as she approached. A single bare light bulb glowed at the end of the small barn and she could make out the shadowy outline of a man sitting on an overturned bucket. She stood in the entrance, the light forming a halo around her slender form, then as she stepped forward, her feet suddenly stumbled to a halt.

"Freddy!"

The short man turned, then grinned.

"Well, now, don't look so disappointed, sugar plum. I ain't such lowly company as all that." He grabbed another bucket, flipped it over, and patted the metal bottom. "Park it right here and keep me company for a spell, dumpling."

"Freddy, I..." She paused, looking at

the friendly, lonesome old face. "All right." She sat down and placed a hand on the mare's neck. "Do you think she'll die?"

"Only the good Lord knows that, honey pot. And He ain't telling the likes of me." He winked, then began a stream of chatter about how the fogger had sprayed for mosquitoes, and anything that came to his shrewd mind. Marlene listened in silence, then when he paused, spoke.

"Freddy' Where's Jesse?"

The foreman shifted the wad of tobacco to the other side of his jaw, then grinned his dark-stained smile. "Shoot! Now, I didn't figure you was down here to visit with old ornery me."

"Oh, that's silly. Of course I . . ."

He held up his calloused hand and shook his stubborn chin. "Never mind the excuses. Besides, I got me a gal." He winked. "And she'd be madder'n a wet hen if she knowed I was talking to another pretty gal."

Marlene laughed lightly. "Then I better not stay too much longer. Where's Jesse? In the other stable?'

"Well, I made the boy go back up the ranch house for some vittles. He hadn't been away from the mare for almost twenty-four hours. Hasn't slept more'n a couple hours a night, too. I told him if he didn't go up and get some nourishment, I was gonna haul off and belt him upside the head bone and drag him up there."

"So he's in the kitchen?" She turned, but her smile dissipated when she saw the dark ranch house. The sole light came from her room.

"No sir. He come back down here and tried to take over again, but I told him to get some sleep or else."

"Then he's in his room?" Marlene said with disappointment, as she rose to her feet and stared at the dark bedroom on the second floor of the house.

"Nope, didn't say that. Say, you want to talk to him something fierce, don't you? Well, I wish I could help, but the boy just up and walked off toting his guitar. Said he had some deep thinking to do. I asked him where he was going this time of night, but he told me weren't none of my business. If I knew where he was, I'd tell you for sure."

"That's all right, Freddy. I think I know exactly where he is," Marlene said. She fondly kissed the old man's head. "Thanks."

"Ah, shoot!" He chuckled, then spat as

she hurried away.

Marlene headed out into the darkness behind the barn. Over the horizon a full moon rose and would soon provide pale light. She paused, her eyes searching the ground for an old path that she once knew so well. Then she saw the trail, now mostly grown over with grass, but still visible to one who knew where to look for it. With a thumping heart she hurried on, until in the distance she saw a whitish structure standing against the ever lighter sky. She stopped and held her breath, then let it out in a long sigh as she heard the soft strains of a guitar and a mellow baritone male voice floating in the cool night air.

A burst of excitement flooded over Marlene and she softly padded down the path again. In a few seconds the words to the old, familiar tune became clear – slow, sad, and full of feeling. Though he carried the tune perfectly, Jesse's voice was tired and raw from lack of sleep, and this gave the words even more poignancy. Stopping a few yards away, Marlene fought back tears. Jesse sat on the grass, his back propped against the worn rock wall of an abandoned well that had been built by Sam Yancy's father over sixty years ago and was made of rusty red sandstone from the local woods. The oak poles that rose from its wall and once held a cross pole to support a pully were gray with age, half eaten by worms, and dotted by woodpecker holes.

Marlene gently sat down beside Jesse and watched his fingers carefully change chords while his thumb moved in slow, easy strums. He finished the song without looking at her, his eyes focused on the distant silky tall grasses to which the moonlight gave an eerie iridescence.

After the last note died away, he gently laid the instrument on top of the old well, whose hole had been boarded up to prevent children and animals from stumbling in.

"How did you find me?" he asked, finally turning to face her. Even in the pale light, Marlene could see the darkness under his eyes and the stubble of unkempt whiskers. In his liquid brown eyes she could see the reflection of the moon.

"You used to always come here when you wanted to think," she answered.

"Jewel used to call it the 'wishing well,'" he drawled. "All the kids, me included, would drop in pennies and make wishes. But this time I guess a whole pocketful of pennies wouldn't help."

"Jesse, please." Marlene shifted her position until she was on her knees beside him. She reached over and took his limp hand in hers. "Vaughn did explain everything to you, didn't he? I mean, about the magazine article. You *do* realize that Vaughn and I aren't getting married?"

Jesse shrugged, then tugged a blade of Johnson grass free and stuck the succulent green stem between his lips. "You'd be a fool not to marry Vaughn."

"What are you saying?" she explained.

"He's got everything a woman could want – looks, money, prestige, security."

"But I don't love him." She put her other hand on his arm and squeezed desperately. His eyes glistened with tears. Jesse looked at her, his eyes growing softer with each second of silence. Then he let go of the blade of grass and slipped his strong hands around her face. With a gentle tug, he pulled her head down until his lips found hers. A soft cry left Marlene's throat as she closed her eyes and savored the warm, tender touch. But when her arms moved to his chest, Jesse quickly pushed them away and climbed to his feet.

"We're just making things worse,

Marlene," he said in an emotion-filled voice. He grabbed the guitar and slung the strap over his shoulder. "You know and I know that you'd be better of with Vaughn. In the city. Anyone can tell how much you love your job."

"Yes, I do love it. But you can't hold a job in your arms at night," she said, climbing to her feet. "I came here to tell you that Vaughn just offered me a promotion to associate editor. I've been thinking all night trying to decide what to do."

"Oh, I see." She saw him avert his eyes to a point above her head. "You'd be a fool not to take it."

"Jesse!" She grabbed his arms and shook with all her might. "Stop trying to shove me out of your life!"

"Look, Marlene, my champion stud and half the brood mares are dying. Do you know what that means? Financial ruin. Years of work down the drain. It would take a miracle to get the ranch back on its feet. Jewel and I would probably be forced to sell. I'd go back to rodeoing, I guess. We'd be exactly where we were six years ago. You didn't stay with me then; why should you now?"

Marlene felt a jolt of pain shoot through her heart at his words, but her desperation pushed aside any pride.

"It's different now. We're older; we know what it's like out there in this crazy, mixed-up world, and we both know that no one can ever make it alone." Her hands planted firmly on his arm, Marlene watched Jesse's face as she spoke. She saw the shadow of doubt clouding his features, reflecting the inner struggle between his conscience and his heart. His eyes glimmered in the moonlight and the night breeze gently lifted the ends of his dark hair, brushing it across his face. Marlene's eyes devoured his handsome features and set jaw. Her arms began to ache for him until her slender frame trembled with desire. Then Jesse's dark eyes softened to the color of black velvet and she knew that something within his heart had won for at least the moment. His fingers touched her cheek, feather-light, traveling to and fro over the smooth line of her jaw.

"I might be back on my feet in a few years ... but ... but I can't expect you to wait around to marry me."

"I don't want to wait to marry you."

The fingers on her cheek suddenly

stopped and a flash of pain passed over Jesse's face. She saw his throat constrict and knew his words were being forced out.

"I don't blame you . . ."

"I mean I want to marry you now, even if you're the poorest man on earth," she corrected him, slipping her hands up to his shoulders.

"Don't be a fool. You'd regret it the rest of your life. I've heard other women say that, only to end up miserable in a few years of back-breaking work. Life on a ranch isn't easy."

"I know."

"Look at you, all soft and silky and delicate." His long tanned fingers lifted the lapel of her silk blouse, then let it drop while his gaze moved down to the expensive designer jeans and boots. "I can't ask you to give up your life-style. You'd be unhappy and I'd hate myself for doing it to you."

"What makes you so all-fired sure that my life in the city is so wonderful, anyway? Maybe life on the ranch would be a blessing compared to living in a lonesome apartment surrounded by strangers, afraid to step out at night for fresh air. Shoot, what fresh air!"

"No, Marlene." He pushed her away, his fingers digging painfully into her arms. For a moment his face registered his surging turmoil, then, he relaxed his hold and looked her directly in the eye. "Marlene, there's something I never told you. It's about my folks – my real parents." He slowly sat on the well ledge. "My mother was beautiful – long black hair and dark eyes. She was from the city and could have had any man, but she fell in love with my father, a farmer. He was a good man, but he was dirt-poor. He was the type that no matter how hard he worked, everything he did more or less failed. I can see him now – tall, too lean, deep ruts carved on his face. And his face the color of leather. I can't ever remember seeing him smile, except when my mother was touching him. They loved each other, but she . . . she just couldn't take the farm life. 'She was meant to be dressed in lace and fancy clothes, sipping tea, not slopping hogs,' my pa used to say. By the time she died, she was wrinkled and ugly. She died from sickness caused by overwork and exhaustion. My father . . ." Jesse paused, staring at his hands for a long time before continuing. "My father died a year later; he just didn't want to go on living without her. And I saw it all." Suddenly Jesse threw his head up, his dark irises glistening with emotion. "God, I loved them both, but love wasn't enough, don't you see? You never were poor, dirt-poor like we were. You just don't know how it kills anything beautiful and breeds misery." He got up suddenly and grabbed the guitar, which he'd laid aside. Marlene felt the tears of desperation starting to blur her vision as Jesse turned and walked away. With the strength of a cornered animal she rushed after him.

"Jesse! Wait! Look, I want to show you something." She tugged with all her power, deriving power and courage from despair. She led him to the other side of the well, and dropped down to her knees, forcing him to join her. She frantically began ripping at the tall blades of Johnson grass and blackberry vines that pricked her fingers. Soon she had cleared away the area, exposing the rock wall all the way to the ground.

"Look," she repeated, pointing a trembling finger to a worn impression carved into the sandstone. Years of rain and inclement weather had smoothed the rough edges, but the shape of a heart and the initials within it still was clearly outlined. "Remember, Jesse? We made love the first time right here. And you carved that heart afterwards and we swore we would love each other forever. We vowed that we would let nothing come before our love. Did all those words mean nothing? Was it all just the game of young foolish kids? Jesse..."

She grabbed his hands, pressing them to her tear-stained cheek. She squeezed her lids tight, but the tears crept from underneath her eyelids, wetting her dark lashes, and when she opened her eyes his face was a blur. She pushed his hands down to her pounding chest. "Jesse, make love to me. And then, if you can still tell me that you can live without me, I'll go back to Dallas and never bother you again. Jesse, please..."

An expression of immense agony covered Jesse's face, and for what seemed an etermity he stared at her, then in a sudden surge of emotion he threw his arms around her waist and drew her against him, burying his face in her hair before he roughly cupped his hand around her face and forced her to look into his misty eyes.

"You know I love you. You know..."

His words faded as his lips found hers, lingering until the tension of their mutual passion reached a burning crescendo. Marlene closed her eyes, relishing the warmth of Jesse's lips and the tender savage strength of his arms drawing her ever-closer to his firm body. She felt the heavy pounding of his heart against hers, and a primitive surge swept through her body, culminating in a throbbing desire in the pit of her stomach.

Silently they began removing each other's clothes until two naked bodies glistened beneath the pale moonlight. They faced each other on their knees, and Jesse's left hand tenderly caressed the curve of her waist and hips while the other stroked her hungry breasts. He leaned over and began burning a trail of kisses down her neck to the tense brown nipples. A soft moan left her parted lips as the swollen breasts received the pleasure of his touch, and her stomach contracted when his hot breath moved over it. His tongue continued down to her receptive thighs and her body instinctively dropped to the soft grass, her fingers reaching for and entwining his dark hair. As the pleasure mounted to an almost unbearable pitch, Marlene pulled Jesse closer. Like a touch of fire, his chest pressed against her breasts and the surging arousal of his manhood pushed against her abdomen. With another groan of pleasure she wrapped her arms around his neck and surrounded his lips with hers. Slowly their bodies rolled together, and Marlene felt the mixed sensations of cold grass beneath her and Jesse's hot flesh above her. While his fingers explored her intimately and his lips lingered on hers, the last salty tears slid from beneath her closed eyelids and clung to her thick, dark lashes like pearls of dew.

Their hearts drummed one another in a passionate, savage rhythm, and they murmured eager words of love and desire in the stillness of the night. The lovers were oblivious to the mournful refrains of the whippoorwill and bobwhites. They were lost in a world of their own making. A world of tenderness, fullfillment, and forgiving. Their desperate lovemaking filled the night until the final release whipped through their bodies and they lay exhausted while the gentle wind soothed and caressed them.

Jesse pulled his shirt over Marlene, then held her to his chest as they lay together in silence watching the moon across the sky.

Marlene adjusted her position so that she could look into his eyes, which were staring unblinkingly at the moon.

"Well?" she said softly. "Was that our farewell lovemaking or the beginning?"

She held her breath, waiting for the reply, and when his gaze met hers, her heart jumped.

"Do you really have to ask?" He smiled softly for the first time in days, and with an irrepressible cry of joy Marlene threw her arms around his neck and kissed his prickly face over and over.

"I'll make you a good wife, Jesse, I swear. I can take the work, I know I can. And no matter how hard times get, as long as we have love..." Her words trailed off as his lips took hers. When he released her, his eyes, though weary, twinkled mischievously.

"All right, future Mrs. Franklin, I'm going to give you the chance to prove those words right now." He pulled her to her feet and tossed her the jeans and silk blouse. "We're going to go straight back to the stables and keep watch over those horses."

"Terrific. We'll talk the night away while we work," she said excitedly.

Rapidly they dressed and then, hand in

hand, strolled to the stables. Inside, the atmosphere of gloom hung heavy, and the silence was unnerving, but even these circumstances couldn't destroy Marlene's happiness. They worked side by side, the way she had always imagined it would be if she married him, and though her bones ached with fatigue and the blisters on her hands tingled with pain, she didn't care.

At five o'clock in the morning, just as the eastern horizon began to turn from black to gray, Marlene dropped to her knees beside Jesse in an empty stall. Their bodies were wet with perspiration and her hair stuck to her neck. It seemed the night breeze had long ago deserted them, but her heart was content. She closed her eyes and leaned back against Jesse's chest.

"Jesse? When will we know ... I mean about the horses?"

"Test results should come in the morning," he replied in a weary, husky voice.

"In the morning," she mumbled, trying to fight off the heavy hand of sleep. "In the morning..." Her words faded and she slumped against his chest. The last thing she recalled was a kiss on her forehead and two strong arms pulling her closer.

Chapter Fourteen

Marlene awakened to the sound of a merry whistle coming from behind her. Slowly she untangled her arms from Jesse's body and stretched her cramped legs. Jesse was breathing deeply, his head still resting against the back of the stall. She knew from the past that he was difficult to arouse from sleep, and the long day and night before had left him exhausted. But, to her surprise, when she placed a long, tender kiss on his lips, they responded, and his hands captured her waist, pulling her near. A light peal of laughter left her throat, feeling warm and good as it rose into the fresh early morning air. She looked down into the deep, warm brown eyes and a wave of love flooded her soul. Gently, she kissed him again.

"Say now, none of that, you two." Freddy's gravelly voice cut through the tingling cool air.

The couple turned, still embracing, as Freddy ambled up to the stall, a wide grin

284

on his face.

"What're you so happy about you old rascal?" Jesse asked fondly.

"Oh, Freddy's got a gal," Marlene teased.

"I know he does," Jesse replied. "How'd she like the ring, Freddy?"

"She's prouder'n a banty rooster, Jess. I'll alway be obliged for all the help you and Red gave me."

"What?" Marlene's mouth fell open and she stared at Jesse. "What ring?"

Jesse smiled down at her, then put his index finger on her nose and tapped lightly.

"I told you that wedding ring you heard me and Bonnie Sue talking about was nothing to worry about."

"But ... I don't understand. Who's your gal, Freddy?"

"Why, Jewel, of course. You don't think I'd have nobody else, do you?" He winked merrily. "I wanted to surprise her with a special ring. The one that belonged to her mother. The old set dropped out of it thirty years ago. I remembered that she always loved that old ring. So Bonnie Sue and Jesse snuck around behind her back getting the set refilled and having the size adjusted to fit her finger."

"Of course, Freddy paid for it all," Jesse added, slapping Freddy's knee.

Marlene felt a relief, a sense of her own foolishness and giddiness sweep over her all at the same time. She glanced at Jesse and saw his warm smiling eyes. He winked and put his arm around her shoulder.

"Feel better now?" he asked softly, then returned his gaze to Freddy. "Well, you never did tell me why you're so all-fired happy, Fred."

"Well, two reasons, besides Jewel saying yes. First, I'm happy because my two most favorite people have finally come to their natural-born senses and got together like the good Lord meant 'em to."

Jesse nodded. "Okay. Thanks, Fred. And reason number two?"

"Oh, nothing much." He paused long enough to shoot a stream of brown juice through the air. "Only that the mare's fever broke and she's up and at 'em, hungrier than a horse, so to speak."

"Th-the mare!" Eyes lit up like Fourth of July fireworks, Jesse dropped Marlene's hand and leaped to his feet. He ran to the small barn at full speed. Marlene jumped up, grabbing Freddy's hand and dragging him after Jesse. They arrived just in time to

286

see Jesse slide to a halt beside the mare, who was now on her feet shaking her crumpled and dirty mane. A lump rose to Marlene's throat as she saw Jesse throw his arms around the glistening neck and press his face against the animal.

"Oh, Freddy, this is so wonderful," she whispered. "Does it mean that the other horses will be okay too?"

"More'n likely. Say, looky here Jess, boy. I wanna show you something mighty interesting. All the while I was sitting on night watch out here I was thinking. I seen the sleeping sickness before and, well sir, something just didn't fit. Specially the fact that only the one stable come down with it. Mosquitoes ain't that picky. Now, do you remember that little fella we always called Shorty? Right after the sickness hit, he run away without collecting his paycheck. Remember me telling you?"

"Vaguely. I guess I was too busy worrying to notice."

"I remember," Marlene said. "You were telling Jesse about Shorty on the night that . . . that he saw the magazine article." She blushed as she caught the look on Jesse's features. But he smiled and squeezed her hand.

"No wonder I didn't hear you talking, Freddy. My blood pressure was hitting the ceiling. But what has all this got to do with sleeping sickness?"

"Well sir, I recollected seeing Shorty mixing the feed in the bin, and he was using a couple of gunnysacks. Didn't mean nothing to me at the time. But then this morning I overheard Johnson complaining how he'd been shortchanged on the hayseed he was supposed to be planting. Came up short a couple bushels."

"Johnson is the man I hire to plow the fields and plant crops," Jesse explained to Marlene.

"Yep. So, while I was sitting here on the bucket, I done me some thinking. Then I done me some snooping, and sure enough, looky what I found." Freddy reached into the stall and withdrew two empty burlap sacks. The bags had large red X's on the front and a warning: NOT FOR CONSUMPTION.

"Here's Johnson's missing seed bags."

Jesse took the sacks gently in his hands, turning them over slowly, his eyes filled with amazement.

"Where'd you find them?"

"In Shorty's bunk, under the mattress.

The way I figure it, he accidentally fed the horses in the new stable this seed. Then, when he seen how sick they was, he hoofed on outa here."

"Damn! If he'd only told me, the vet could have treated them and all this work and worry..." Jesse paused, shaking his head sadly.

"But ... I don't understand," Marlene interrupted. "What difference does it make? It was just seed, wasn't it?"

"Not exactly," Freddy explained. "The seed fer planting is treated with chemicals to keep them from rotting and getting ate by varmints. Poison chemicals. When a horse or cow eats the seed, they get sick. Now, a horse can't throw up, so he just has to wait fer the poison to go through his system. Then he's fine and dandy, if he hadn't ate too much poison."

"Thank God," Marlene threw her arms around Freddy, kissed his prickly chin, then turned to Jesse. She could see the relief flooding his face as he looked over at the crisp white stables. In the east, the first fingers of dawn were painting the sky pink, and off to their left the sound of horses racing down the track rose and fell with the rhythm of their hooves and the urging of the exercize boys.

"Come on, Marlene, I think what we need is a deep drink of fresh air and a cool dip in the old Brazos." Jesse's arms circled her shoulders and firmly steered her toward the old stables where the healthy horses were kept. He swiftly saddled two horses and they rode in the direction of the river a few miles away.

"I do this every morning, real early like this. I've often thought how much better it would be to have a . . . a wife alongside me to talk to."

"It's a terrific habit, Jesse," Marlene said in an emotion-filled voice.

"Do you think you could get used to it?"

"Oh, yes, yes. I'm used to it already."

Jesse laughed lightly, then grew quiet, and Marlene's heart began to pound in anticipation of his next words.

"Well, uh, you know it's a far cry from the city life you're used to. Just because the herd's out of danger doesn't mean things will be smooth sailing. Times get rough – floods, droughts, tornadoes – just about everything you can think of happens sooner or later. I can't promise you that it'll be easy being married to me."

"I never doubted that a minute, Mr.

Franklin," she teased, reaching over and tweaking his elbow. But his quick, almost shy side-glance made her relaize he was worried about something. He sucked in a deep breath.

"It won't be like being married to an oil millionaire's son, either."

Marlene's face went pale for a brief instant, then she laughed lightly.

"Well, thank goodness for that. I hated golf, tea parties, and all that phoniness. Every time I dove into that tile-lined swimming pool that reeked of chlorine, I would think about the old Brazos and wish I were right in the middle of it, being bit by minnows and fighting off the frogs and turtles."

Jesse threw back his head and roared with laughter, then jerked the reins back. He stared into her eyes a long loving moment, then twisted in the saddle and extended his lean muscular arm.

"Well, here you are, lady. It's not the cleanest swimming pool in town, or the bluest, but, by damn, I bet my boots it's the longest." With that, he swung his long legs over the saddle and dropped to the ground, then lifted Marlene down in one graceful movement.

The stood side by side looking out over the green river waters that shimmered with the pink tinge of dawn's first light, its smooth surface dimpled by leaping fish. Marlene studied Jesse's profile as the breeze softly lifted his hair and the mellow light gave a golden tint to his calm features. She saw the love in his dark eyes as they slowly scanned the landscape below – the river and the miles of rolling green hills. Then she saw him watching two tiny specks of gold that represented car headlights along the distant highway. The merry chatter of mockingbirds was so loud that she could not hear the buzz of the motor or the hum of tires as the vehicles rumbled over the metal bridge spanning the Brazos. When she looked again at Jesse, he was staring at her with a serious countenance. Quickly he glanced away.

"Not much traffic out here since the Interstate opened," he said. "Gets mighty lonesome sometimes."

"I never particularly cared for the noise of the city, if that's what you're hinting at. I was born and raised in Waterford, remember?"

Jeesse threw her another quick glance, then pushed his hat up on his brow and shifted his legs.

"It's not exactly the city life I was thinking about."

"No? Y-you aren't getting cold feet about marriage, are you?"

"Of course not, but ... I've been thinking some more, and ... well, any fool can see how much you love writing for that magazine. And you're good at it. I'd hate to think that all your talents would be wasted out here. Suppose you began to get restless and regret it. There's no work in Waterford to keep you challenged. I don't imagine the *Daily Herald* needs any reporters for all the excitement going on in town." He smiled, the worry still showing in his eyes.

"I've been thinking about that too, Jesse. Turning down an associate editor's job was no snap decision. But for a long time now I've been wanting to become a free-lance writer. I know lots of people in the business and I have a million ideas in my head for articles, starting right here with one about a quarter-horse ranch."

As Marlene waited for Jesse's reply, her heart thumped faster. In silence he took her hand and they climbed down the bank and then strolled along its gentle curve. Marlene removed her shoes and the soft sand felt icy cold on her bare feet when she stepped up to the river. The cool liquid lazily lapped her toes while she waited for Jesse to remove his boots. He joined her, still in silence, and Marlene waited anxiously for him to speak.

"Jesse," she finally asked softly, "is everything going to be all right?"

Jesse studied her green eyes. Then he placed his hands on her shoulders and pressed lightly.

"Maybe," he said with a slight touch of tension in his voice. "That depends on one thing."

Marlene searched the depths of his dark eyes.

"Oh?" she asked in a trembling voice. "What?"

"Will you be my girl?" A smile flickered on his lips, then as he saw the uncertainty in her eyes, he added, "For the rest of my life."

A wave of love washed over Marlene and she threw her arms around Jesse's neck.

"All my life that's all I really ever wanted to be – Jesse's girl," she replied as her lips found his warm, hungry mouth.

The smell of the damp earth and tangy wild grasses combined to form a perfume so sweet that it filled her senses to the point of bursting. From treetops and telephone wires overhead came the soft, beckoning cooing of mourning doves. And as the sun peeped its orange-yellow head above the horizon and Marlene felt the first touch of heat on her cheek, she knew that this was where she was always meant to be. The delicious pressure on her lips deepened, and Jesse, flexing his knees, gently pushed her down to the cool sand and drew her closer and closer until nothing existed except the pounding of his heart and his warmth and his love.